I0718131

Foolish Heart

Book Nine, MacLarens of Fire Mountain
Contemporary Western Romance

SHIRLEEN DAVIES

Books Series by Shirleen Davies

Historical Western Romances

Redemption Mountain
MacLarens of Fire Mountain Historical
MacLarens of Boundary Mountain

Romantic Suspense

Eternal Brethren Military Romantic Suspense
Peregrine Bay Romantic Suspense

Contemporary Western Romance

MacLarens of Fire Mountain Contemporary
Macklins of Whiskey Bend

The best way to stay in touch is to subscribe to my newsletter. Go to my Website *www.shirleendavies.com* and fill in your email and name in the Join My Newsletter boxes. That's it!

Copyright © 2017 by Shirleen Davies

All rights reserved. No part of this publication may be reproduced, distributed, or transmitted in any form or by any electronic or mechanical means, including information storage and retrieval systems or transmitted in any form or by any means without the prior written permission of the publisher, except by a reviewer who may quote brief passages in a review. Thank you for respecting the hard work of this author.

For permission requests, contact the publisher.

Avalanche Ranch Press, LLC
PO Box 12618
Prescott, AZ 86304

Foolish Heart is a work of fiction. Names, characters, places, and incidents are either products of the author's imagination or used fictitiously. Any resemblance to actual events, locales, or persons, living or dead, is wholly coincidental.

Book conversions by Joseph Murray at
3rdplanetpublishing.com

Cover design by Sweet 'n Spicy Designs

ISBN: 978-1-941786-50-5

I care about quality, so if you find something in error,
please contact me via email at
shirleen@shirleendavies.com

Description

She walked away once. Now she's back. Too bad someone may want her to disappear for good.

Ernesto Salgado's life continues to change. An ex-Special Forces operative, he recently left the U.S. Marshals Service to start a new life—minus the woman who left him without an explanation or backward glance. Working as head of security for MacLaren Enterprises is the opportunity he needs to move on.

Paige Wallace made a choice that continues to haunt her every day and each night. The life she dreamed about, had at her fingertips, disappeared in one decisive moment. A new job with her longtime friend offers the break she needs, a chance to forget her biggest failure and start over.

No problem, right? Except Paige and Nesto now work for the same company.

And that's not the only issue. The family member she dropped everything to help has become embroiled in illegal dealings, doing business with those who would harm not only Paige, but the entire MacLaren family.

As head of security, Nesto's priority is to keep all employees and owners safe. He'll do whatever needs to be done to excel at the job, even when it includes protecting the woman who walked out of his life.

The more he digs, the deeper the threat becomes, affecting everyone. Nesto has to face a hard truth—the only way for him to succeed is with Paige's help.

How can he trust a woman he thought loved him but walked away, especially when they acknowledge the passion still burning between them?

As the threat increases, Nesto uses all the resources available to protect those he cares about. If he could only use the same resources to protect his heart.

Foolish Heart, book nine in the MacLarens of Fire Mountain Contemporary western romance series, is a stand-alone, full-length novel with an HEA and no cliffhanger.

Foolish Heart

Prologue

Lightning flashed across the sky a few seconds before a thunderous crack ripped through the nearly silent night. The deafening sound occurred three times in as many minutes, stalling Ernesto Salgado's attempt to complete the tie around his neck. He couldn't remember the last time he'd worn a suit. His job as a U.S. Marshal didn't require the use of formal wear, not even when transporting high-profile prisoners across the United States—or the world.

Nesto's hands shook as he finished the knot, then smoothed the silk fabric down his white dress shirt. He knew the shaking wasn't due to the storm, a rare event in this southern California community.

Opening a drawer, he pulled out the small box hidden below his t-shirts. It had taken him a few weeks to pick the right ring, but months to build up the courage to present it to the woman he planned to marry.

Looking at his watch, he sucked in a slow breath, glancing in the mirror.

Grow a pair, Nesto, he thought before picking up the keys to his truck and heading to the back door of the three bedroom house he'd purchased last year.

He and Paige had been together over two years when he bought the house. It was a big step for a man who'd sworn to never marry, a bachelor who lived for his work.

After years in Army Special Forces, obtaining a college degree along the way, he'd passed the U.S. Marshals Service exam with ease. His total time working for Uncle Sam gave him the opportunity to retire within a few months. Nesto knew he'd stay until they kicked his ornery butt out the door.

Grabbing a hat at the last minute, he slammed it down on his head, then ran the short distance to his driveway. For months he'd planned to buy a raincoat, one of those trench-type coats men wore in Chicago and New York. Other stuff always got in the way. He didn't even own an umbrella, figuring he'd lose it before they had enough rain in San Diego to warrant pulling it out of the closet.

Pushing the unlock button on the key fob, he drew open the door and jumped inside, brushing the rain from his suit. He started the engine, revving it a few times before backing into the street to make the short drive to Paige's apartment near the university.

Nesto repeated the words he'd been rehearsing for weeks, his hands gripping the steering wheel tight enough to cause his knuckles to whiten. Who would've ever thought a boy from Montana, growing up dirt poor, would be lucky enough to have a woman like Paige Wallace fall in love with him? From a wealthy family, a PhD framed in Brazilian rosewood and secured to the wall in her office at the university, she had her pick of men. She'd chosen him and fallen hard, the same as he'd done.

The rain let up as he cut the engine in front of the large complex of rentals. Hurrying up the long walkway and into the lobby, Nesto punched the button to her floor, taking another deep breath. His plan was to take her to dinner at an upscale restaurant overlooking the harbor. Reservations had been confirmed weeks before, guaranteeing a quiet table in the corner with a sensational view. Standing outside her door, he told himself not to jump the gun and ask her on the drive along the water.

Swallowing what he refused to believe was fear, Nesto knocked, then stepped back. He could hear Paige's voice inside the apartment, figuring she must be on the phone. Knocking harder, he forced himself not to use the key she'd given him a year ago. He wanted this night to be special from beginning to end. Be a gentleman, giving her a night to remember. An instant later, the door opened.

"Nesto?" Her brows knitted together in a frown. "You're early." She wore her favorite jeans, a light pink V-neck top, and tennis shoes. He couldn't remember the last time he'd seen her so frazzled...or so beautiful.

Stepping forward, he pulled her close for a deep kiss. Paige responded as she always did, with instant heat and passion. Kicking the door closed, he deepened the kiss, both moaning into each other's mouths as desire streamed between them. It had been over a week since they'd been together, his job taking him to multiple states.

As his hands roamed over her back to settle on her hips, he felt her tremble. A slight smile turned up the corners of his mouth until the tremors turned to shaking, a quiet sob breaking from her throat. Drawing back, he rested his hands on her shoulders, watching as her normally cheerful face twisted in misery. Her sudden movement away had his chest squeezing.

"Sweetheart, what's wrong?" He took a step forward, his arms outstretched in front of him, stopping when she held up a hand. Her gaze darted behind him, causing him to look over his shoulder. Two suitcases sat next to the door, along with her computer case. Turning back to her, Nesto's gaze narrowed. "What's going on?"

"I thought I'd be gone before you arrived."

"Gone? Where are you going?" Taking a quick glance around the room, his breath caught at the emptiness. Gone were the framed photos of the two of them. Cards he'd given her for no specific reason had been removed from the shelves on one wall. Clenching his fists at his sides, he waited.

"I'm so sorry, Nesto. So, so sorry."

A knock on the door stalled his response. In an angry move, he gripped the handle, yanking the door open. A young man, probably a college student, stood in the hall.

"Did you call for a ride?"

Nesto felt something shift inside him, although he wouldn't figure out until much later what it was—his heart shattering.

"Yes, I did." Paige walked forward, avoiding Nesto as she pointed to her bags. "Those by the door. I'll take the computer case." She bent to pick up the bag.

Nesto grabbed her arm, doing his best to keep the fear out of his voice. "Where are you going?"

She looked at the young man. "I'll be right down."

He nodded before picking up the bags and leaving.

Nesto waited until she looked up at him, swiping at tears streaming down her cheeks. "Paige? Tell me what's going on."

Shaking her head, she looked away, unable to hold his intense gaze. "I'm going home."

"Home? This is your home, in San Diego, with me."

"I'm so sorry." She bent to pick up her computer, tensing when he wrapped his large hand around her wrist.

"Stop saying you're sorry and tell me why you're doing this." When she didn't respond, refused to look at him, he spun away, shredding both hands through his hair. Pacing down the hall toward the bedroom they'd made love in more times than he could count, he took a deep breath. His life felt as if it were falling apart and she wouldn't speak to him, wouldn't explain.

"This wasn't planned, Nesto. I'd never do anything to hurt you." Her soft voice ripped through him, her words meaning nothing.

Turning, he stared at a woman he thought he knew, the only woman he'd ever loved. "Then why go?"

"I don't have a choice. I'd never leave you if..." Her voice trailed off as her throat clogged in pain. Placing a hand over her mouth to stifle another sob, she turned from him, rushing down the hall to the door.

Nesto started to go after her, halting when she opened the front door. "Is there anything I can say to change your mind?" He thought of the ring in his pocket, a future without her.

Her head bent in resignation, her body shaking with emotion, she let out a shaky breath. "I'll always love you, Nesto. There'll never be anyone else." Pausing, she took one last look at his beautiful face, eyes full of compassion...and pain. "Never anyone else..."

His heart froze as the door clicked shut behind her.

Chapter One

MacLaren Enterprises
Fire Mountain, Arizona
Two years later...

"On a scale of one to ten, what is the risk to us from the cartels?" Heath MacLaren, Chairman of MacLaren Enterprises, focused his razor-sharp gaze on Ernesto Salgado, Vice President of Security. After several threats over the last few months from two of the most notorious drug cartels in Mexico, the safety of employees at all operations became a top priority.

Nesto didn't try to sugarcoat his assessment. He glanced at Heath's brothers, co-CEOs Rafe and Jace, before his somber expression locked on his boss. "An eight or nine."

Jace sat forward, resting his arms on the conference table. "It's been almost two months since what happened in Texas and there hasn't been any retaliation. Sounds like you believe they'll still come after us."

Besides the three brothers, the heads of each division, plus a few others, joined them for what had become a weekly security meeting. Never in the history of the company had the threat level been so high or lasted for such an extended period. It made life even crazier for the firm, which offered bucking stock for rodeos, horse breeding and training, ranch resort vacations, ranch services, and real estate acquisition and management. The brothers' appetite for expanding the company hadn't come close to being sated.

"As Kade will attest, the cartels have long memories and endless money. When the time is right, they'll strike back." He glanced at his boyhood friend and Rafe's oldest son, Kade MacLaren, head of the bucking stock division.

Kade reached for one of the bottles of water on the table and opened it. "It isn't unusual for them to associate themselves with other groups, such as a motorcycle club. In exchange for guns, money, or drugs, the club will carry out whatever retaliation is agreed to with the cartel. It isn't a partnership of allies. Neither trusts the other, but they'll work together, as long as it benefits both." He nodded at Nesto to continue.

"There is always the chance the cartels will forget about us, decide we're not worth the effort. They know MacLaren Enterprises isn't a threat to them. Some of our people happened to get caught in the middle of an internal dispute. My recommendation is to keep the current level of security for a few more weeks, then reassess."

Heath cleared his throat. "Thanks, Nesto. Questions anyone?" When no one responded, he adjourned the meeting.

Kade filed outside with Nesto, checking the time. "How about a beer before you head home?"

"Sure, man. I've got nothing planned. I'll follow you."

They ended up at the Tavern, a local hangout they'd been to many times since Nesto left the U.S. Marshals

Service and joined Kade in the family business. Since the organizational changes about a year ago, Kade split his time between offices in Crooked Tree, Montana, Cold Creek, Colorado, and Fire Mountain, Arizona. It made for a hectic schedule, but he thrived on the fast pace and demanding agenda. Finding a couple stools at the bar, they ordered beers.

"Is Brooke in town?" Nesto referred to Kade's wife and Heath's stepdaughter, who traveled between locations as part of her job with the company.

"Nope. She'll be back this weekend, then we'll fly up to Montana. Why don't you come up for a few days, do your inspection a little early?"

"No can do. My calendar is booked solid right now." Pulling out his phone, Nesto checked his schedule. "I'll be in Crooked Tree in two weeks. How about I stay with you and Brooke for the weekend?"

"Yeah, about that…" Kade's eyes narrowed on Nesto, taking a sip of beer. "Have you talked to Paige since she came out for the wedding?"

Nesto cocked a brow. "And why would I talk to her? I couldn't get away from the reception fast enough after she showed up. She only came to Fire Mountain because you and Brooke announced the fact she's pregnant, and Paige didn't want to miss it—them being best friends and all. I heard she flew back a couple days later. In and out, done deal." He looked at the television mounted above the bar, then back at Kade. "Besides, what does that have to do with me staying with you guys a couple days?"

Kade hunkered over his glass of beer, not meeting Nesto's eyes. "Guess you haven't heard the news."

"Ah, hell," Nesto muttered. "Tell me it's not what I'm thinking." He knew how generous Heath, Rafe, and Jace, or *the brothers*, as most called them, were when it came to handing out jobs to family or those close to them. It was how he got his position.

Kade shook his head. "Wish I could. The brothers offered her a job and she accepted. Starts next week."

"And she'll be staying with you and Brooke." A churning began deep in his belly, burning upward, squeezing his chest.

"Yep. She'll also be working with Brooke. Paige's doctorate is in a similar subject matter. She taught at the university and has been doing consulting since moving back east. Seems she's ready to head back west."

Nesto's jaw clenched. He couldn't think of anything to say, other than to spout his dismay. Who the MacLarens hired wasn't his business.

Kade shifted to look at him. "She'll work with Brooke for a week or two, then head to Fire Mountain."

The hope Nesto had that she'd be living in Montana, far away from him, faded. "She'll work out of headquarters."

"Afraid so, brother. Brooke needs help on a high level. There's no better choice than Paige."

Nesto signaled the bartender for two more beers, along with two shots of whiskey. "It would've been nice if Heath had mentioned something to me."

"He didn't remember you and Paige being together. You were in San Diego and broke up months before leaving the marshals and moving to Arizona. He never put two and two together."

Nesto let out a frustrated breath, his voice growing louder. "And *Brooke* didn't think it important enough to bring up?"

"No." Kade picked up the whiskey, tilting the shot glass toward Nesto, then downing it in one swallow. "She and I had strong words with each other after I found out."

Nesto winced at the thought of them arguing, one defending Paige, the other supporting him. Still, the entire situation irked him. "Brooke is one of the smartest people I know. She had to have known how hiring Paige would play out with me." Shaking his head, he drank his whiskey, setting the glass on the bar with more force than necessary. "Why would she do it without saying anything to me? At least I could've been prepared."

"You're hearing about it now, bro. Besides, you know how Brooke can be when it relates to people she cares about. Paige is like a sister, and you're like a brother." Kade looked away, but not before Nesto caught something in his eyes, causing a flash of understanding.

"*Please* don't tell me she's trying to work a deal to get Paige and I back together."

The corners of Kade's mouth tilted up, even as he worked to keep his features neutral. "I didn't say that."

"Ah, man. Tell your wife to stay out of this. Whatever Paige and I had or didn't have is over and done. Brooke needs to accept it, the same as me." Finishing his second beer, he considered ordering a third, then took a breath, wishing he could change the decision Heath had already made. "Damn, Kade. What's a man to do?"

Kade's smirk died when he saw the devastated look on his best friend's face. Until the latest MacLaren wedding, Nesto had been doing great, moving forward, pushing thoughts of Paige from his mind. Now they were in the forefront again, a shining mess to face each day. Clasping Nesto on the shoulder, he squeezed lightly.

"Accept she'll be around. You'll run into her at headquarters sometimes, maybe be in the same meetings. Be your normal, professional self, and don't let her get to you. Better yet, find someone else. Nothing like a new woman to shove away mistakes of the past."

"I tried that. After she left, I hit whatever woman showed an interest."

"And?" Kade asked, although he thought he already knew the answer.

"Waste of time. It helped for a few hours, then it all came rushing back."

"Might be different if you meet the right woman. Guess you won't know until you try. Well, I've got a standing phone call with Brooke." Kade pulled out some money, leaving it on the bar.

Standing, Nesto did the same. "I'll head out with you."

Outside, Kade turned to Nesto. "Look, don't overthink this. Give it some time. I'm sure it will all work itself out after a while." Slapping him on the back, Kade took off.

Climbing into his truck, Nesto gripped the steering wheel with both hands, staring straight ahead. He had the perfect job, working with his best friend and people he admired and trusted. The money was excellent, and he couldn't ask for a better boss than Heath MacLaren. Screwing this up wasn't an option.

Blowing out a shaky breath, he started the ignition, accepting Kade's advice. He'd bury whatever feelings he once had, showing Paige a professional front, treating her with respect, the same as he'd do for anyone. He'd faced enemies in the past and always survived. This would be the same. Paige might have once been the woman of his dreams, but no longer.

Philadelphia

"I don't understand why you can't stay here and build a life. You could find another teaching position, continue your consulting, maybe meet the right man." Irene Wallace wrung her hands together, a gesture she'd never do in public, where everyone saw her as the consummate matriarch of a socially prominent family. "There are plenty of fine, eligible men for you to meet. You might even fall in love."

Continuing to place folded clothes into her luggage, Paige kept her back to her mother, refusing to be drawn into another discussion about staying in Philadelphia. She returned for a reason, doing what she could. In the end, it hadn't been enough.

"Have you seen my hoodie, Mother?" Placing her hands on her hips, Paige glanced around the room. "I swear I left it on the chair in the corner."

Walking to the closet, Irene drew it off a hanger, handing it to her daughter. "You know how Mary is about clothes not being put away."

Paige couldn't stop the grin at the mention of the woman who'd run the house since a few years after Paul's birth. When Irene's social obligations kept her out much of each day, Mary had become almost like a second mother to Paige and her younger brother, continuing to make her presence known after both children had left.

Where are you, Paul?

The thought flashed through Paige's mind before she could push it away. Forcing herself to focus on the task at hand, she rolled the sweatshirt, using it to fill the space at the upper edge of her carry-on. Studying the other two bags, her gaze cut to the closet.

"Mother, I may need to have Mary ship some things out to me. I'll label them before I leave so she'll know what to send."

"I suppose it's too much to ask you to stay a few more weeks. Your father hasn't had as much time to spend with you as he'd like."

Paige rolled her eyes. She wanted to point out her father would have plenty of time if he didn't spend most of it with his mistress—the woman he thought he'd hidden so well. In many ways, Paige thought it good she and her mother had learned of the woman on a shopping trip in the city, spotting the two of them having lunch, holding hands, talking in intimate whispers.

"With all that's happened since my return, we never had a chance to talk about Father and, well..." As soon as she voiced her thought, Paige wished she hadn't. The color drained from her mother's face, her hands clenching until her knuckles appeared white.

"There's nothing to discuss. I've learned to live with the many choices he's made during our marriage."

Paige's voice softened. "I shouldn't have brought it up. It's your decision on how to handle issues with Father. It's just that I want you to be happy."

Irene's back straightened, a new gleam in her eyes. "You don't have to worry about my happiness, sweetheart."

Paige stopped in the middle of zipping closed a bag and stared at her mother. "You don't intend to leave him, do you?"

Walking to the window, Irene gazed out on manicured lawns, well-pruned bushes, and pristine walkways. The back yard where she'd held so many garden parties, taken so much pride in designing, now seemed to be one more sad reminder of what truly mattered. Her son had disappeared, Paige was leaving, and her husband had emotionally and physically separated himself from her years ago.

"What would make you ask that, Paige? I've been in love with Peter since graduating from college. He's provided a good life, everything I could ever dream of having..." Irene caught her lower lip between her teeth before she said more than she should.

Paige's chest clenched at the melancholy in her mother's voice. A woman who'd always been so full of life and love. She wanted to see the light in her mother's face again.

"Come with me."

Irene's eyes widened, a flash of something Paige hadn't seen in a long time showing in her expression before she concealed it. "Oh, I couldn't. Not with the big fundraising event coming up and your father's trip after that."

Her throat tightened on the last. Paige knew he hadn't invited her mother to go along on the three week business trip through Europe.

"There's no reason you can't come for a visit while Father is gone. By then, I'll be in Fire Mountain at one of the MacLaren cabins. It has two bedrooms—plenty of room for both of us."

A wistful expression crossed Irene's face before disappearing. "I've never been on a trip without your father."

"Well then, that's another reason you should come. He'll be gone for three weeks. The perfect opportunity for you to take your first trip alone." Paige walked up to her, taking Irene's hands in hers. "Think about it. I'll be staying with Brooke for a couple weeks before going to Fire Mountain. You'd have a chance to meet the MacLarens. You'll love Annie, Heath MacLaren's wife."

"Perhaps." Irene drew her hands away. "I may not make a decision until the last minute, though. You never know about your father. He might change his mind and ask me to come along."

Paige's heart ached for her mother, knowing it wouldn't happen. Although they didn't speak of it or have any proof, they both knew Peter planned to take his mistress, an insult so great, Paige didn't know how her mother accepted it with such serene grace.

"If not, I'll expect you to fly out."

Setting the luggage on the floor, Paige took one more look around. "I believe everything is packed."

"Are you sure I can't drive you to the airport?"

"I'm sure. Believe me, you don't want to fight the traffic." Looking out the window, she saw the cab coming up the drive. "The car is here."

Paige felt a pang of remorse at leaving her mother this time. When she'd left years ago, it had been to obtain her doctorate in San Diego. Paul had still been at home, and her father had come home most nights. She hoped her mother would consider visiting. If nothing else, it would get her out of this big empty house that seemed more like a prison than a place of refuge.

Paige rested against the plane's window, closing her eyes as the pilot reached his designated altitude. Her thoughts skipped between her brother, the reason she'd come home, and her mother, a woman who'd always been strong and steadfast in her love for her husband. After all his progress, Paul had chosen to walk out one night, leaving the family who'd come together to help him. He'd gone underground, cutting all ties to those he knew.

She hoped her mother would decide to visit. Getting away from Paige's father, letting him know his wife could survive without him, might just be the kick he needed to realize what he seemed determined to throw away. Regardless, it had been years since her mother had ridden a horse, spent a day having fun.

Hearing the soft hum of the engines, her thoughts turned to Nesto, a man she would never be able to forget. Even though she'd given him ample warning, he'd been angry when Paige showed up at the ranch, refusing to speak with her or even acknowledge her presence. It had been awkward when he'd walked away, leaving her stunned and raw with pain. Not that she blamed him. Good intentions and solid reasons for her walking out on him might never overcome the resentment or hurt she'd caused.

Over the last weeks, she'd faced her share of doubt about accepting the job at MacLaren Enterprises. If it had been offered by anyone else, she would've refused. Brooke knew how to wrap it all up in a nice little bow and present the package to Paige. Perfect job, outstanding pay and benefits, great working environment, and a boss she already loved as a best friend.

Brooke had assured her, given the various travel schedules, running into Nesto would be a rare occurrence. For some reason, Paige didn't believe that was entirely accurate. As the plane moved closer to its destination, her stomach churned with uncertainty. She'd be working for Brooke, who reported to Heath, the same as Nesto. Odds were their offices wouldn't be too far apart. Paige couldn't stop wondering if she'd made an enormous mistake by accepting the job.

"May I get you coffee, water, or a soft drink?" The flight attendant leaned over, getting Paige's attention.

"A diet cola." Paige hesitated a mere instant. "And rum."

Chapter Two

Crooked Tree, Montana

Paige stepped onto the tarmac, a broad smile breaking across her face at the sight of Brooke jumping up and down, waving, a more somber Kade standing next to his wife. Her welcome committee.

"I can't believe you're actually here." Brooke ran forward, wrapping Paige in a warm hug, then stepping back. "We are going to have so much fun."

"I'm so ready for that."

Kade walked up, giving her a brief hug. "You might have to squeeze in a little work every now and then."

Paige laughed. "I'm ready for that, too. I didn't expect to see you here, Kade."

Slipping her arm through his, Brooke smiled. "This is where my husband gets territorial and controlling. He's hardly let me out of his sight the last few days. After we return to Fire Mountain, my days of traveling will be limited."

Walking to the terminal, Kade held the door open. "It isn't just me. Heath and Annie feel the same."

Paige turned to Brooke, lines of worry creasing her forehead. "Is it the baby?"

Brooke nodded. "The baby is causing the doctor some concern."

Kade tilted his head to the side. "*Some* concern? What he said was you need to take it easy and not be hustling around the country, putting stress on yourself and the baby."

"Or?" Paige asked.

Brooke sighed, knowing Kade had valid concerns. "We could lose him."

"Well then...wait...it's a boy? When did you find out?"

"Yesterday. I have doctors in Crooked Tree and Fire Mountain, so we opted for the sonogram here. Kade burned up the phone lines around the country last night." Brooke stopped in the baggage area, placing a hand on her stomach. She glanced at her husband. "I think he kind of wanted a girl."

Kade snorted. "Only because I know the kind of trouble boys get into."

"And their toys are expensive," Brooke added, thinking of the Harley, tricked-out truck, quad, and other equipment her husband kept in Fire Mountain.

"There is that." Kade smiled.

"You're going to be great parents, whether you have a boy or girl. I'm betting there will be a couple of each running around your place before you're done." A sudden jolt whipped through Paige, causing a split second of intense pain around her heart. She and Nesto had spoken several times about children, deciding on at least three, maybe four. Placing a hand on her chest, she pushed, trying to reduce the pressure.

"Are you all right?" Brooke asked.

"Fine. Ate some spicy food for lunch and it's catching up to me." The lie came easily. She'd told herself so many since leaving Nesto, rationalizing her decisions had become common. "Those are my bags." She pointed to the two matching red suitcases.

"I've got them." Kade strolled away, leaving them alone for the first time.

"You look great, Brooke. Amazing, actually. How's Kade doing?"

"He's been wonderful. Nothing seems to faze him. Well, he may have lost it for a second when the sonogram tech pointed out why she knew we were having a boy." Brooke smiled, remembering the look of pure joy on his face. "He's worried about me right now, so he's hovering a little more than usual. That's okay. I sort of like having him close."

"Who wouldn't? You won the prize with Kade."

Brooke studied Paige's face, seeing so many emotions flitter across her features in the span of a few seconds. "Thanks for taking the job. I know it was difficult knowing you'd be facing Nesto."

"It won't be difficult. You saw the way he reacted when he saw me at the wedding reception. He hates me. I'd feel the same if I were in his place."

"You never told me why you left him, Paige. I keep telling myself you must have had a good reason for walking away, but—"

"You two ready to head home?" Pulling two red bags behind him, Kade stopped next to them.

"Lead on." Paige picked up her carry-on, glad for the interruption. She didn't want to share her true reasons for leaving, particularly not to her close friend and her ex-DEA agent husband. When she'd made the decision to walk away from Nesto without explanation, it had been to keep him protected from the actions she had to take. Until she knew the whereabouts of her brother, and the trouble he may still be in, nothing had changed.

Fire Mountain

"Hey, Gage. I was just going to call you to see how things are going." Nesto placed a stack of files aside. Gage Templeton and Skye MacLaren, Kade's oldest sister, were engaged, planning to marry in a few weeks. An ex-saddle bronc and bareback champion, he was now an executive with Double Ace, a supplier of bucking stock, partnering with the MacLarens on larger rodeos.

"I've been in and out, keeping up with business while trying to work with Skye on the wedding plans long distance. I keep pushing for Vegas, but she's not biting." He chuckled. Gage had been through a rough divorce, vowing to never marry again. After some ups and downs, Skye had succeeded in piercing his defenses.

"At least it's at the ranch. You know Annie and the other ladies will do all they can to help."

"That's what I'm counting on. If it were me, we'd marry at city hall, go on a honeymoon, then have a blowout celebration everyone would remember."

"I hear you, man. Get it done." Nesto knew he'd want the same if he were in Gage's place. If he'd still been with Paige, she'd have agreed, eager to get on with the party. Clearing his throat, he directed the conversation to a safer topic. "How's it going at Double Ace?"

"Good. Glad we signed the agreement to have you provide our security. Between you and Thad Montgomery's contacts, we're doing a lot better than a few months ago."

Double Ace and MacLaren Enterprises agreed to a contract allowing Nesto and his team to provide security and risk management services for a year. Afterward, the two companies would assess the situation and go from there. The main advantage had been to give the brothers peace of mind. Once Skye and Gage married, she'd move from Crooked Tree to his home in Houston, using an empty office at Double Ace for her work at MacLaren Bucking Stock, the division run by her oldest brother, Kade.

"How's Thad doing? Haven't heard a word from him, although I think he keeps in touch with Kade." Nesto had worked with Thad during some troubles at Double Ace. The same as Kade, Thad was an ex-DEA agent, working freelance now. Nesto had a pretty good idea what that meant.

"Moving to the Hill Country, near Austin. He's picked up a couple new clients in the area. Fell in love with the place and bought a house with land. It's what you can do when you're a bachelor." Gage didn't sound the least bit remorseful.

"Hey, it's not too late to change your mind, break it off with Skye."

"Hell no. I know what I've got and there's no way I'm letting her go."

Nesto chuckled into the phone. "Good answer. If you'd said anything else, I would've had to fly out and rough you up until you regained your senses."

"And you're just the man to do it."

"Damn straight." Nesto checked the time. "I need to get to a meeting. Call if you need anything." Pocketing his phone, he headed down the hall to one of the smaller conference rooms. Feeling the cell vibrate, he pulled it out, smiling when he saw Kade's name. "Hey, bro. You having a slow day and decided to harass me?"

"When have you ever known me to have a slow day? Harassing you doesn't sound too bad, though."

"I'm headed for a meeting. Can I call you later?" Nesto waited, wondering about Kade's hesitation. "You there?"

"Yeah. I just wanted to let you know Paige arrived." Kade didn't sound pleased, making Nesto wonder if his friend had opposed the idea more vigorously than he'd let on.

"Okay. So you've warned me. That it?" He wanted to sound casual, disinterested—everything he wasn't at the moment. The mention of her triggered an ache he'd never been able to erase. Nesto didn't know what he'd do when she reported to her office at headquarters, but he had to get himself under control.

"Plans have changed. She was supposed to work with Brooke here in Crooked Tree for two weeks. Heath called and wants both of them in Fire Mountain the first of the week. The company is looking at an acquisition and needs their input."

Nesto leaned against the wall, taking a deep breath. This wasn't welcome news, but he couldn't afford to let anyone, not even Kade, know how much her being hired affected him.

"Doesn't matter to me when she shows up."

"So no worries on your end?" The concern in Kade's voice didn't surprise him. They'd been through more than a few tough times together, relying on each other when they'd had no one else. Confiding in Kade about the breakup had been natural, a way to vent the pain he hadn't been able to shove aside on his own.

"No worries, man." He owed Kade for the job at MacLaren, which had been a true lifesaver. No way would he let his friend down. "The work I do doesn't overlap with Paige's, so it's doubtful I'll run into her for weeks." *At least a man can hope*, he thought, straightening to continue toward the conference room. "Gotta go. And, Kade, thanks for the heads-up."

Opening the door, he saw everyone already seated, involved in their own conversations. All except Heath, who stood, motioning Nesto to follow him into the hall. Something about the set of his boss's jaw warned him to keep his emotions in check. Heath pinned him with his legendary stare, his face devoid of expression.

"You've heard about Paige Wallace joining the company?"

He didn't flinch under the unyielding gaze. "Yes, sir. Kade informed me a week ago."

Heath seemed to study Nesto's face before continuing. "I assume you don't have an issue with her being here."

"No issues at all, sir. If Brooke says she's the best for the job, I'll go with that."

Heath clasped him on the shoulder. "If there are any problems, you come to me and we'll work something out. I have no intention of losing you, Salgado. Do we understand each other?"

Nesto let out a breath, his shoulders relaxing. "Yes, sir. There's no need to worry. I've got it handled."

"Good. Now, let's finish this meeting so everyone can get on with their weekend."

Crooked Tree, Montana

"I really hoped we'd have some time to catch up before being thrown into the craziness at headquarters. But once the brothers set their sights on a new acquisition, all energy is focused in that direction until a final decision is made." Brooke sat at the table in the house she and Kade rented near the Crooked Tree office. She and Paige had worked from here today while Kade took care of business at the bucking bull stock location.

"Craziness in a good or bad way?" Paige drank her second diet soda, picking up a chip every now and then, taking notes when needed.

"Definitely good. There's a lot of energy, people working together to dig into the company the brothers want to purchase. This time, it will be a little different. Heath's son, Trey, has joined the company and will be getting indoctrinated into how things work."

"He was in the navy, right?"

Brooke nodded. "Trey and his wife, Jesse, graduated from Annapolis and were fighter pilots, or as Trey corrected me, Naval Aviators." She chuckled, remembering his good-natured teasing. "They got out a few months ago and moved to Fire Mountain with their son, Trevor. And they're expecting their second child. The general buzz is Trey will someday take Heath's place, but who knows. He may hate it."

Paige's brows furrowed as she made a design on her pad of paper. The family dynamics she'd lived through were nothing compared to the huge MacLaren clan with almost everyone having some role in the business. The closeness of working together intrigued her. The politics of a family business...not so much.

"Do you expect trouble with him coming home?"

"None. Everyone knew there'd be changes when Trey returned. The interesting part will be if he likes being cooped up in an office after flying jets for years." Brooke rolled the glass between her palms, thinking of her oldest stepbrother. "He's incredibly bright and energetic. I think it will be great to get some fresh perspective on the plans the brothers have put in place."

"Do you know much about the company they're thinking of buying?"

"I wish I did. Heath, Rafe, and Jace have been unusually quiet about this one. They haven't even let on what industry it's in."

Paige glanced up. "Kade doesn't even know?"

"Nothing. We'll all be at the meeting and hear about it at the same time. Then it will be eighteen-hour days until a decision is made."

Paige smiled. "Right. As if Kade or Heath will let you put in those kinds of hours."

"Which is why Heath wants you in the meeting and on the acquisition team from the beginning."

Biting her bottom lip, Paige studied the scrawls on her paper, the design showing no meaning.

"Do you think Nesto will be involved?"

Brooke reached over, covering Paige's hand with hers. "You can plan on him being in most meetings. If it weren't for the pending acquisition, you might not see him for weeks. I know you hoped for more time..."

Paige shook her head. "No. It's fine. I just want to know what I'll be walking into. The fact Nesto will be there isn't a problem. It's better to get any awkward moments out of the way up front rather than having it fester. We're both professionals, Brooke. We'll be fine."

A memory flashed through her mind of the night she walked away from Nesto, the stricken look on his face that almost had her changing her mind. Ignoring her father's request hadn't been an option—at least that was what she'd thought at the time.

She thought of her father's pleading voice and all the unknowns with her brother, Paul. They'd been so close when they were younger, her being his protector until his size and weight surpassed hers. Within a year of her leaving for college, his life started to fall apart. She'd helped as best as she could, but it hadn't been enough.

Her life had changed because of his choices and the inability of her and their parents to get through to him. She'd left an excellent job and the man she loved to help Paul. Now it seemed it had all been in vain. After months, she and her parents thought he'd reversed his negative slide, then Paul disappeared, leaving them angry and confused. Two private investigators hadn't been able to trace him, all their leads turning into dead ends.

Even though her parents would've been glad to have her stay with them in Philadelphia, the time had come for Paige to return to her own life. She continued to work with one of the investigators, hoping for some sign of her brother. Each day without news had become harder to bear. The job at MacLaren Enterprises would provide the stimulus she needed to keep her mind off the dread of not knowing, keep her focused on what she could control. The job, however, didn't come without risks. The biggest one being to her heart.

Chapter Three

Fire Mountain, Arizona

Eric Sinclair, Heath's stepson, and Mitch MacLaren, another of Rafe's sons, sat at a corner table of the Tavern. Paying little attention to the noise around them, they waited for several other members of the family to arrive, along with a few friends.

The men didn't often meet for drinks on weekends, unless they and some of the other MacLarens went on a trail ride or rode their motorcycles. Unless congregating for a wedding or other occasion, the changes in the company made it a rare occurrence for them to all be together at one time.

"There's Cam now." Eric nodded toward the entrance, seeing his older brother walking in with Trey. Nesto and Matt Garner followed a couple minutes later. "I heard Kade won't be in town until tomorrow."

Mitch nodded as the other men took seats around the table. "I spoke with him this morning. He, Brooke, and Paige Wallace arrive in the morning. From what he says, your sister will be staying at the ranch until the baby comes."

"No kidding?" Cameron Sinclair, Brooke and Eric's older brother, sat next to Mitch, signaling the bartender for a round of beers for the table. "Brooke didn't tell me she had to stop her activities."

Mitch shook his head, his signature taciturn expression evident. "Hey, I'm just the messenger. You'll be able to grill Kade as much as you want tomorrow."

Cam took his beer, nodding his thanks to the waitress. "Paige Wallace? Is that the woman Heath hired to work with Brooke?"

Matt and Eric glanced at Nesto, seeing his body tense, even as his face held no trace of discomfort.

Trey took a sip of his beer, then set the glass down. "That's her. She and Brooke met while both attended the university in San Diego. A good buddy of mine has been going out with Paige's cousin, Shelley, for years." He shook his head. "Well, off and on anyway."

"One of your flying buddies?" Eric asked.

"Yeah. You met him when Jesse and I married. Ryan Cantrell. He's a helluva pilot. Wouldn't surprise me if he stayed in the navy until he retired."

Nesto listened as the conversation moved from one topic to another, his mind unable to let go of the fact Paige would be working a few offices away within two days. If it weren't for the mandatory meeting the brothers called about the acquisition, he'd have already flown out to one of the other MacLaren locations. One week a month, he stayed at the headquarters in Fire Mountain, leaving the other three weeks to travel between the different subsidiaries.

"Your Harley fixed yet, Nesto?"

His head shifted toward Mitch at the mention of his name. "Fixed and ready to roll. You have a place to ride?"

"Kade mentioned putting together a ride tomorrow afternoon."

Eric leaned back in his chair, crossing his right ankle over his left leg. "Mom will want all of us there for lunch." His mother, Annie Sinclair, had married Heath MacLaren a few years before, becoming the matriarch to the ever-growing family. "She's already got it all planned out." He looked at Mitch and Cam. "She's got Dana, Lainey, and Amber helping her."

"My wife loves that stuff," Cam said, thinking of Lainey.

"So does, Dana. Although we eat out more often than she cooks." Mitch accepted another beer.

Eric chuckled, an image of his wife crossing his mind. "Amber and I are the same."

"Yeah, but you two love to cook," Cam said. "Like the rest of us, you just don't have time."

Trey's expression sobered as he glanced around the table. "Does anyone know anything about the acquisition? Pop, Rafe, and Jace are unusually silent about it."

Matt sat forward, resting his arms on his legs. "They haven't said a word to me. From what Kade says, he's in the dark, too. Cassie asked Heath straight out. He told her she'd have to wait, the same as the rest of us."

"Well, if he won't tell your wife—his own daughter—he sure isn't going to say anything to anyone else until Monday." Mitch rubbed the back of his neck, then smiled when his younger brother, Sean, walked in. "Hey, buddy. Didn't expect to see you today." They shook hands, then hugged, slapping each other's back before Sean dropped into the last empty chair, taking the beer Trey handed him.

Taking a long drink, Sean shook his head. "I'm telling you boys, that dude ranch is making me crazy." He grimaced as they all laughed, Trey and Matt patting his back. "I'm not kidding. Do you have any idea what it's like to work around families who've never been close to a horse before?"

"Or the groups of single women looking for an experience with a *real* cowboy?" Matt smirked.

Sean grimaced. "You'd know all about them after all those years avoiding the buckle bunnies on the rodeo circuit."

"Who says I avoided them?"

Trey sent him a warning glare. "Don't let Cassie hear you say that. I think she's in denial about what your life was like before you two got back together. You don't want to go spoiling her image of you."

Matt nodded, lifting a brow. "Yeah. There is that." He sipped his beer, glancing over the rim of his glass at Nesto. "You're quiet tonight."

Blowing out a breath, he smiled, although nothing about his current situation seemed amusing. "Just listening. What can I possibly add to tales about a dude ranch, flying jets, or the rodeo circuit?"

Matt shook his head. "Don't give me that. I've heard you and Kade talk. There's nothing boring about your stint in Special Forces, your work as a U.S. Marshal, or Kade's time with the DEA."

"Old stories from another life, man. I've left it all behind to work with you jokers."

"Meet any new girls since coming to Fire Mountain?" Sean asked. Before Mitch met and married Dana, the two of them used to go out seeking female companionship on Friday nights.

Nesto grinned. "Not that I'd tell you about."

Eric snapped his fingers, looking at him. "That's right. Didn't you and the new employee, Paige, used to go out?"

Blowing out a breath, Nesto shifted in the chair, his face clouding over. "Like the rest of my life, she's old news."

The table quieted, the strained silence ending when Cam stood up. "We'd better get going if we're going to meet the ladies for dinner."

Mitch glanced at his watch, finished the rest of his beer, then stood. "I'm with you. Come on, *girls*. You too, Nesto. No lame excuses about how you have to be somewhere else."

As much as he didn't feel like it, Nesto followed them outside. He'd spent enough nights alone since learning about Paige being hired. Tonight might be one of the last times he'd be able to join the MacLarens without worrying about her being present, and he planned to enjoy it.

They filled the largest table available at the local steakhouse, taking up a third of the space. Heath, Rafe, Jace, and their wives begged off, but everyone else expected at the meeting on Monday had made it, except for Kade and Brooke...and Paige.

Nesto took a seat between Mitch and Trey, placed an order for a ribeye, then settled back to enjoy the Malbec he'd ordered. He'd gotten hooked on the Argentine wine a few years before when he and another U.S. Marshal had been tasked with escorting a well-known international arms dealer back to the United States. Although he had loved the job, he was thankful those days were in his past.

Cam cleared his throat, getting everyone's attention. "I know we're all curious about what Heath, Rafe, and Jace will announce at the meeting. There's no sense ignoring it, so my suggestion is we go around the table. Anyone who wants to make a guess should go for it."

"Another dude ranch." Matt leaned forward in his seat, smirking at Sean, who glared back at him.

"Oh, hell no. I'm not dealing with any more tenderfoots than I already am."

Matt didn't give up. "How about a dating service you can run in your spare time. I heard *Get It Together* is on the market."

Sean shook his head, taking a sip of his drink. "It's *Get Together*, and I'm not dealing with anything having to do with more single women."

Nesto jumped in. "That mean you're not up for making the rounds after dinner to check out the newest ladies in Fire Mountain?"

"I could be persuaded," Sean chuckled. "Any other *good* guesses?"

"A western clothing firm," Amber suggested.

Mitch shook his head. "Only if it includes outdoor wear for other sports. Unless you're talking about one of the major jean manufacturers, and the odds of that are slim."

"There's a horse breeding facility in Colorado Jace mentioned a few months ago." Cassie took a sip of iced tea, then narrowed her gaze at Mitch. "I didn't think much about it at the time, but maybe he had a serious interest in it."

Nodding, Mitch looked at Cassie. "Maybe. I do know they want to expand the breeding business. What better way than to buy an existing operation."

The conversation slowed as the waiters set their food before them and they began to eat. After a few minutes, Eric narrowed his gaze at Cam.

"Heath and Rafe have talked about establishing a finance company for our own projects. I've never thought it made sense, but maybe they've found a way to make it work by acquiring an existing firm."

Cam nodded. "If it fits the business model, they'll find a way to incorporate it into the company."

Skye set down her fork, leaning forward in her seat. "What about Double Ace?"

Matt's brow lifted. "What about them?"

Gage Templeton, his closest friend, and Skye planned to marry in a few weeks. He was also one of the key people at Double Ace, headquartered in Houston.

Skye nodded at Cam. "As he said, they go after companies that fit our company. Even with the troubles over the last few months, Double Ace is profitable, has been an excellent partner in our bucking stock operation, and their business model works well with ours." Shrugging, she picked up her glass of wine. "Just a thought."

Her brother, Sean, leaned toward her. "And a good one. I hadn't thought about bringing them into the fold. I mean, with you and Gage marrying, and Ivan Santiago already related to the MacLarens, I'm surprised a merger hasn't come up before now."

Eric leaned back in his chair, crossing his arms. "Maybe it has and we just weren't part of the conversation."

"Huh," Matt mumbled to no one in particular. "Seems it wouldn't require all of us to fly into town for something the size of Double Ace."

"Maybe there's more to it than we think." Cam leaned toward Lainey, whispering in her ear, then laughing at her response.

"Do you think Skye's right, Cam?" Cassie asked, taking the dessert menu from the waiter.

He nodded. "I think it makes sense. I also believe Matt is right. Seems it wouldn't take all of us to review acquiring them. There's got to be something we're missing."

Nesto relaxed back against the chair, rubbing his chin, doing his best to appear interested in the conversation. The trouble was he couldn't get his thoughts off the woman flying into town the following day.

He'd struggled for months after Paige left him standing alone in her apartment in San Diego. She hadn't even given him the courtesy of a backward glance or a word of explanation. The engagement ring concealed in his pocket had taunted him long after she'd disappeared, a reminder of the fool he'd been to pin his future on a woman. Since then, he'd been incapable of anything more than casual flings and one-night stands. They'd seemed to be enough, until he'd learned of her new job at MacLaren.

Nesto had always relied on his instincts. Right now, they told him the best defense against any weakness in front of Paige would be a strong offense. He'd already committed to visiting one of the local hangouts with Sean. Nesto would suggest the new bar he knew to be a favorite of a woman he'd gone out with a handful of times.

Tall and slender, she wore her long, dark red hair twisted into an intricate knot, giving the impression of being stiff and reserved. He'd taken a chance one night, buying her a drink, then dinner, accepting her invitation to follow her home. They'd repeated the routine the next few weeks before work sent him out of town. Although their encounters had been unplanned, he enjoyed her easygoing style, detached conversations, and uninhibited sex with no strings. When he returned, he had every intention of calling her—until Kade dropped the bomb about Paige. Now might be the time to renew his connection to the leggy redhead.

The change in tone of the conversation pulled his attention back to the table. Several had stood, talking in small groups, ready to head home.

"You ready to head out?" Sean stood next to him, as if he'd been able to read Nesto's mind.

"Always." Standing, he nodded toward the others before turning to walk outside. "Do you have a car?" He sure hoped so because Nesto had every intention of not sleeping in his own bed tonight.

"Pop's letting me use his truck. He bought Reyna an SUV and is trying to teach her how to drive."

Nesto shook his head, chuckling. He'd known Kade's mother for years, remembering the time he and Kade had tried to teach her to drive. "I've never known a person more unsuitable to sit behind a wheel than Reyna. I sure hope Rafe knows what he's doing."

"Not a clue. Pop will do anything for her."

Nesto glanced at Sean, wondering if Rafe and Reyna's marriage bothered him. "You ever hear from your mother?"

Sean winced at the question. "That's a conversation for another time. Tonight, I'm ready to relax, laugh, and have some fun. You game?"

Clasping Sean on the shoulder, he nodded. "I'm right with you, my friend."

Chapter Four

Paige unpacked her bags, setting clothes on the bed as she looked around the bedroom of her new home. The MacLarens kept several cabins close to the main ranch house. With the continual expansion in the family, they'd built a few more this past year.

Each had two bedrooms, a bath, full kitchen, eating area, and living room with a rock fireplace. Spaced up to a hundred yards apart, they provided housing for family and friends.

Paige had no problem picturing herself on the covered porch, watching sunsets with a glass of wine and a book. The problem was the fact Nesto lived in the cabin closest to hers, his front door no more than forty yards away.

Walking to her bedroom window, she glanced out just as a dark gray pickup came to a stop in Nesto's driveway. She held her breath, chest tightening when the man she'd dreamed about every night for months stepped out, then looked directly toward her. Panicked, she jumped away from the window, hoping he hadn't spotted her staring.

Sucking air into her lungs, Paige inched back toward the window, hoping he'd gone inside. Instead, she watched as he ran a hand through his hair, then settled a cowboy hat on his head. Reaching into the back seat, he pulled out a small case. A sharp pain sliced through her, recognizing the overnight bag he always kept in his car, ready to spend the night at her place before they'd decided he should keep clothes at her apartment.

He'd started carrying it because of his job, never knowing when he'd be given orders to escort a prisoner from one place to another. Now that he'd left the U.S. Marshals Service, the fact he still carried it told her more than she wanted to know.

Dropping her gaze, Paige noticed the top she'd been holding twisted in her tight grip. Forcing herself to relax, she tossed it on the bed, then sat down, wondering why she'd put herself in this position. It hadn't gone well when they'd seen each other at Rafe and Reyna's wedding. Paige knew this wouldn't be any easier.

A sharp pounding had her jumping up, her heart racing as she made her way to the door. Pulling it open, her eyes widened before she instinctively took a step backward at the harsh look on Nesto's face.

"They put you in *this* cabin?" He glared at her, not a hint of welcome in his voice or stance.

"Hello, Nesto. You're looking...well."

"You can't be here. I'll go ask Annie to find you another place." Turning, he stormed away, jumped into his truck, and drove off before she could explain there were no other cabins available. According to Annie, all were occupied, except the one right next to Nesto.

Closing the door, it wasn't fifteen minutes before she heard the rumbling of his truck again. Expecting him to come back over, maybe even apologize for his rude behavior, she opened the door and stepped onto the porch. Getting out of the truck, he cast her a cursory glance before disappearing into his own cabin, a scowl marring his handsome face. She wouldn't be getting that apology.

Sighing, she walked back inside, dropped onto the sofa, and buried her face in her hands. His initial reaction didn't bode well for them working together. Living next door would be impossible.

Paige knew she and everyone else had been invited to Annie and Heath's for a late lunch. From what Brooke had told her, it had become a Sunday tradition for any family in town, including friends and employees staying in the cabins.

Stretching out, she laid her head on a throw pillow, closing her eyes. An image of Nesto and her on the beach, holding hands, smiling as they strolled along the shore, warred with the fierce image of her new neighbor. Her heart squeezed at the contrast. Hatred radiated in his expression, and rightfully so.

If she could, Paige would wipe out all of the last two years, returning to her life in San Diego and the love she shared with Nesto. So many plans had been cast aside because of one panicked phone call from her father.

She'd been determined to tell him no. At some point, her father had to stop relying on her to deal with Paul and his choices. She'd done everything possible to keep him off drugs, escorting him to rehab more than once before being accepted into the doctorate in California.

Paul had finally kicked his habits, then turned his talents toward what he believed would be a more lucrative venture—manufacturing and distribution. Her parents had discovered a piece of his small empire when they'd visited one of their properties.

Behind their large vacation home, hidden in the basement of a century-old brick building, they found a lab—unoccupied, but operational. As an executive in his own firm, a man who'd never tasted any type of illegal drug, her father knew they were looking at trouble.

Peter Wallace took his wife home, then visited their other two vacation houses, both on large plots of land and concealed within thick stands of trees and foliage. To his disgust, he found several unknown cars hidden in the trees, people moving in and out. He didn't have to go inside to know what he'd find.

Paul had brought more trouble to her family, and their father wanted Paige to fix it.

Her family had always known about Nesto's job as a marshal and Kade's background with the DEA. After serving their country in the military, they'd spent years battling crime, drugs, and corruption. Her brother was now a supplier, operating labs and distribution from family property. If they learned of her brother's activities, Paige knew the government could seize everything her family owned. She couldn't put Nesto in that position.

Paige stuck to her initial reaction, telling her father she wouldn't leave Nesto to help her miscreant brother. Then he'd done the unthinkable—put her mother on the phone. The sound of her mother sobbing, her broken voice pleading for Paige's help, broke her resolve. It was the toughest decision she'd ever made.

And now she'd pay for it.

Nesto slammed the door behind him, took a deep breath, then cursed as he stalked to the kitchen. Taking a beer from the refrigerator, he chugged it down, glancing at the clock. Eleven in the morning. He couldn't remember the last time he drank before noon.

Setting the empty bottle on the counter, he pulled out another cold one. He had three hours before facing Paige at the MacLaren's and he meant to have all the fortification he could get. At least he'd thought that until the glass touched his lips.

Setting the bottle down, he rested his hands on the counter, leaning forward, hanging his head. Getting drunk wouldn't help and may even make things worse. Nesto thought he'd been prepared to face Paige at the wedding reception. One look at her confirmed he wasn't.

He'd been a jerk, realized it even as he stood facing her, responding to her presence months ago much the same as he had today. Like facing any enemy in the past, Nesto needed to formulate a plan on how to work, and live, alongside the woman he still loved more than his own life. To do that, he had to learn why she'd left, leaving a hole in his heart too big to heal.

He'd hoped staying tangled up in the sheets last night with a woman he enjoyed would provide a shield against the pain her being close still caused. Not even the beautiful, long-haired Valerie, or her uninhibited response, had rid him of his need for Paige.

"Hey, brother. You in there?"

Shaking his head, Nesto pushed away from the counter. Drawing the door open, his face broke into a grateful smile at the sight of Kade.

"Wondered when you'd be knocking on my door." Reaching out his hand, he tugged his closest friend into a hug. "You have time to come inside for a bit before heading to the ranch house?"

"That's why I'm here." Following Nesto, Kade took in the neat interior, noting some new framed photographs. "You've made some improvements." He gestured toward the wall of art. "Did you take these?"

Nesto held out a beer, touched his bottle to Kade's, and nodded before he took a sip. "Yeah. Once in a while, Heath gives me some downtime. I usually ride one of the horses out a few miles. I see something different each time."

Kade studied the images. "These are good. Did you ever consider showing them in one of the art galleries in Fire Mountain?"

Nesto threw his head back, a deep laugh escaping. "Hell no. Have you been in one of the galleries lately? The work of those photographers is phenomenal. I can't even compare their work to what you're looking at here. These are for me."

"Maybe, but that won't last long once Brooke sees them. She'll insist on having a few framed for our cabin." Moving to a chair, he sat down, stretching out to cross one long leg over the other. "Look, about Paige—"

Nesto held up a hand, stopping him. "Don't go there. Besides, I get it. Brooke needed someone and Paige is the perfect choice."

"Don't feed me that bull. We both know having her here is going to tear you apart, mess with your mind the same way it did when she left. You've got to talk to her. Find out why she left, then put it all behind you."

Dropping onto the sofa, Nesto took a long drink. "Won't work. First, we aren't speaking, at least not more than two or three words at a time. Second, I no longer care about her reason for leaving. Paige made her choice and that's it."

Kade's gaze narrowed on Nesto, his close friend and a man he'd trust with his life. Studying the firm set of his jaw, the cold glare in his eyes, he had no doubt Nesto wanted to believe the words. More so, he *needed* to believe them.

"If you say so, brother." Draining the bottle, Kade stood up, heading to the kitchen. "Tell you what. Instead of you and me hanging around after lunch, let's saddle our horses and take a long ride. You can take more of these *average* pictures."

Joining Kade at the door, Nesto slapped him on the back. "You're an ass, but I'm still willing to ride with you."

"Good. See you at the ranch house."

Nesto leaned against the doorframe, watching as Kade climbed into his truck and took off. He fought the urge to look at the neighboring cabin, even as he wondered what Paige was doing, if she might be thinking of him. The instant his thoughts went in that direction, Nesto shoved them aside. He didn't need to go down that road...not ever again.

"It's great to have you working for us, Paige." Heath gave her a brief hug, his other arm around Annie. "I know you were supposed to have a couple weeks working with Brooke before getting thrown into the fire, but things change fast around here."

"No worries at all. I'm excited about the opportunity." Paige sipped the soda she'd gotten when she walked in the door.

The house overflowed with family and friends, a sight that warmed her heart. She'd always longed for a large family of her own, hoping it would happen with Nesto. At the thought of him, the man materialized, walking through the front door with the supreme confidence she'd found so captivating when they first met. Making his way to the center of the room, he spared her a cursory glance, his face devoid of expression, as he accepted a beer from Kade, laughing at something his friend said. Her gaze shifted back to Heath when he spoke.

"Tomorrow morning, you'll have time to see your office before the meeting. Anything you need, talk to Brooke or me. I want you to be comfortable."

"Thanks, Heath."

"Hey, Paige." Cassie walked up, giving her a hug. "It's so great having you here." She glanced at Heath. "Don't let my dad intimidate you. He's a lot of bark with little bite."

Heath wrapped an arm around his daughter, kissing her forehead. "Who says I don't have any bite?"

Cassie laughed. "Ask anyone in the room. They'll all give you the same story. Okay if I take Paige away for a bit? The ladies want some time with her."

Dropping his arm, he nodded. "No problem. Make sure you ladies eat your share of the food Annie's prepared."

"Has that ever been a problem?" Cassie slipped her arm through Paige's, guiding her to a patio off the living room.

As they walked past the others, Paige's eyes locked on Nesto's for a split second before his smile faded and he looked away. She didn't have time to consider how to react before her phone rang. Pulling it from her pocket, she excused herself, moving toward Heath's office.

"Hello?"

"Hey, Paige. It's Paul."

Nesto watched as Paige took her phone and disappeared into Heath's office. He couldn't help wondering who was on the other end. Her parents, worthless brother, maybe a boyfriend. The thought of her with someone else hadn't been a serious notion. At least he hadn't allowed it to be until now.

Excusing himself, he walked toward the office, unsure of his intentions. Getting closer, he paused when he heard Paige's raised voice. Nesto had heard the same tone before—a mix of anger and confusion, a woman trying to stay calm when all her instincts screamed for her to shout. Curious, he moved closer, trying not to seem obvious to the others standing twenty feet away.

Paige's hand shook as she held the phone to her ear. "How the hell did you get this number?"

"What? You don't want to talk to your own brother?" His voice dripped with sarcasm, sending her tension skyrocketing.

"Where are you? I've been desperate with worry. I even hired an investigator to look for you."

"Bad idea, Paige. Look, I know the folks found some stuff at their places."

She shook her head, rolling her eyes. "*Stuff.* Is that what you're calling the crap you're into?"

"I don't know what you're talking about, sis. I'm a businessman, nothing more. Anyway, that's not why I called."

Sucking in a breath, she steadied herself against Heath's desk. "I don't understand."

"I've set up a new business arrangement, and it's out your way. Thought maybe we could meet and catch up."

The tone of his voice shook her. She'd heard it before. Each time he'd lied to her about something. "What kind of *business arrangement*?"

"Thought I'd explain it all when we get together. Later this week work for you?"

At one point, a call from Paul with a request to meet would've been good news. No longer. "Look. I know what you're into and I want nothing to do with it—or you. I gave up my life to help you, and for what?" Taking a breath, she rubbed a hand across her forehead. "You've made your choice. Don't even consider involving me."

Paige hung up, reeling from the call. Before talking with him, she and her parents had no proof Paul actually owned the labs they'd found on their properties. He'd disappeared before they could confront him. Now her heart sank, knowing the truth.

The sweet boy she'd protected growing up had buried himself so far down the rabbit hole, she'd never be able to pull him out. The truth stung. He manufactured and sold meth, and who knew what else, on property owned by her parents. They could lose everything if the feds discovered the operations on their land.

Not only had Paul put himself in a reprehensible position, but when his actions were discovered, he might very well take the rest of his family down with him.

Chapter Five

Nesto moved away from the door, rejoining Kade and the others around a table loaded with chips, salsa, and other appetizers. Keeping his back to the office, he glanced over his shoulder to see Paige walk out, her face ashen.

He'd heard enough to know she was in some kind of trouble. It shouldn't matter—he didn't *want* it to matter. Paige's business was her own and he wouldn't allow himself to care.

"Paige." Kade waved her over. "There are some people I don't think you've met." Ignoring the scorching look Nesto sent him, he wrapped an arm around her shoulders, introducing her.

"Glad to meet you, Paige. Welcome to the company." Sean shook her hand, followed by the others.

"Heard you're staying in one of the cabins." Mitch looked at Nesto, clasping him on the shoulder. "Annie said you're in the one next to this miscreant. Let us know if he gets to be too annoying and we'll have a word with him."

The smile on Paige's face faltered before she pulled herself together. "I don't think you have to worry. He and I go way back. Right, Nesto?" She locked her gaze with his, daring him to argue.

Staring at her, his jaw tightened as he nodded. "Sure. Way back."

Several of the men glanced between the two, keeping silent as their gazes narrowed.

"Have you had a chance to get with the girls?" Kade asked.

"Not yet. I'm headed their way now. Good to meet all of you." She didn't look at Nesto as she made her way past several other people before disappearing outside.

Kade watched Nesto's gaze follow Paige out the door. Placing a hand on his shoulder, he turned him toward the bar.

"Another beer?" Kade reached into the undercounter refrigerator, pulling out two bottles, handing one to Nesto.

"A whiskey would be better, but yeah, I'll take it."

Both remained silent as they took a few sips, watching the others mingle. "At least you didn't walk away from Paige this time. It's a step in the right direction."

Shaking his head, Nesto looked through the window at the group of women. He couldn't take his gaze off Paige—her beautiful face, laughing eyes. There was something else in her expression, though. Strain, a pinched look he'd seen before, and sallow skin few, except Nesto, would notice.

He thought of the phone call, her frantic voice, then hard resolve before she hung up. In all the years they were together, he'd seen her this way only a couple times and both involved her brother. She knew Nesto's opinion of Paul and her numerous attempts to help a brother who didn't care about her or her family. Still, he understood. Family came first, the same as it did for the people gathered today.

"Okay, boys. Steaks and burgers are ready to grill." Rafe looked around the room. "This is your time to shine."

"Or crash and burn," Sean called out, invoking the others to slug his arm or pop him upside the head. Ducking, he moved away. "Hey. Just telling it like it is."

Mitch held up his beer, tipping it toward him. "Little brother, if you're going to whine like a girl, I'd suggest you stay in here with the women and toss salads. Leave the grilling to the real men."

"Not a chance, bro," Sean laughed. "Someone's got to baste the meat."

"All right. Enough banter. It's time to work." Heath walked into the room holding a tray loaded with raw meat.

"We're on." Kade nudged Nesto, who set his empty bottle on the counter, not taking his eyes off Paige. "Let's eat, then saddle our horses. I'm ready to get out of here."

Paige sat next to Brooke, doing her best to down the food on her plate. The tension churning in her stomach, causing the meal to taste bitter, didn't surprise her. Between Paul's call, Nesto's surly manner, and general nerves about starting a new job, all she wanted was to go back to the cabin, take a long bath, and go to bed early.

She'd been on an emotional roller coaster far too long. The call from her parents over two years ago, then leaving

Nesto behind, had triggered a series of disappointments with little to boost her spirits. Blaming herself for the way she'd walked out, then her failure to help Paul, sat heavy on her heart. If she could go back, do it all again, she'd refuse her parents' request, forcing them to deal with her brother on their own. Paige wondered if she'd held firm, would she still be taking quick sidelong glances at Nesto sitting at the far end of the table, or would she be next to him, a ring on her finger. Kade's voice jolted her back to the present.

"Sorry to cut this short, but Nesto and I have plans."

Mitch looked at Kade. "And what would those be?"

"A long trail ride, and no, you aren't invited."

"Ah, that's sweet." Sean held up his glass. "Here's to male bonding."

Brooke stifled a chuckle. Kade had already mentioned his plans, getting her full support. He and Nesto rarely had time to themselves, and she knew how much the friendship meant to each of them. She turned toward Paige.

"How about we help Mom clean up, then we can go into town with the girls. I need some more maternity clothes, and there's a new shop in the mall I want to check out."

Paige didn't feel much like shopping, but the expression on Brooke's face forced her to change her mind. "Sounds good."

"Great. I'll borrow Mom's SUV so we can all fit. I know Jesse and Cassie want to come." She leaned closer.

"Plus, Lainey is pregnant. She called me last week after she and Cam found out."

"That's wonderful." Although she barely knew her, Paige felt genuinely happy for Lainey, even as a hard knot of longing settled in her chest. "Have they announced it to the rest of the family?"

Brooke started to speak, then closed her mouth when Cam stood up, grabbing Lainey's hand.

"As you all know, Matt and Cassie, Trey and Jesse, and Kade and Brooke are pregnant. Not to be outdone, we'd like to share that Lainey and I have also entered the same club."

Congratulations and general commotion at the announcement gave Paige the opening she needed to excuse herself. Seeking a few minutes of solitude, she walked inside, making her way to the back of the house where a large family room held hundreds of books, games, and a large screen television. Walking past the bookcases, she ran her fingers over the titles, not so much to select one as to distract her from her shaky emotional state. By the time she returned to the table, she hoped Nesto and Kade would've left for their ride.

"Paige?"

Her heart thudded in her chest at the sound of the voice that could send heat raging through her body. Fingers stilling on a title, she dropped her arm, turning to face Nesto. She found it hard to breathe when her gaze locked on the hard, yet vulnerable look on his face—an expression she hadn't expected.

Clearing his throat, he moved closer. "Are you all right?"

She found it hard to form the right words. She wanted to lash out at him for his boorish behavior, at the same time wanting to rush into his arms, find comfort in his touch. Instead, she stayed put.

"I'm fine." Clasping her hands together, she raised her chin, refusing to look away. She had no intention of giving him the satisfaction of chipping another hole out of her already tenuous state.

Nodding, his throat worked, the vein in his neck pulsing, as if he wanted to say more. Instead, he turned away.

Paige didn't want him to leave, but couldn't bring herself to confide in him. "Um...thanks for asking."

Pausing for an instant, he looked over his shoulder. "Sure."

Lowering herself into a nearby chair, she buried her face in her hands. At this moment, she hated her brother with an intensity beyond anything she could've ever imagined. Worse, she hated herself. She'd been so focused on helping Paul and keeping Nesto out of trouble by knowing about her brother's actions, she'd lost touch with what made a true relationship.

No matter what obstacles they faced, Nesto had always stood with her. In so many ways, he let her know his devotion held no limits, his love no boundaries. All she had to do was ask and he'd be right there with her. Instead, she'd made all the wrong decisions. In her mind, they were for the right reasons, but none of that mattered now as his footsteps echoed down the hall.

Nesto would find a way to work with her, tolerate Paige's presence, but she'd never feel his arms around her or hear his whispered words of affection. Those were buried in the past, along with his love for her.

MacLaren Enterprises

Paige walked into the conference room Monday morning, scanning the table for Brooke, spotting an empty seat next to her. To her relief, Nesto hadn't arrived, which gave her time to settle in without his intense gaze.

After the shopping trip, she'd begged off dinner in favor of a long, hot bath. She'd bought cheese and wine while out with the ladies—enjoying them while taking a long soak. She wrestled with what to do next. It hadn't helped that Paul had tried to reach her again and she'd ignored his call.

Drying off, she slipped into her robe, poured another glass of wine, and settled on the sofa. The view through the picture window captivated her, making it easy to get lost in the beauty of the Northern Arizona mountains. She understood why Brooke loved it here.

Taking a deep breath, she forced herself to consider how to move forward. She'd give her job a hundred percent, do what she'd trained for, and make a place for herself in the company. Dealing with the other issues were more complicated.

A tortuous hour later, after allowing her mind to consider one option, then another, Paige finally made a difficult decision. It didn't give her peace, but offered hope, which was all she would allow herself to expect.

"All right. It appears we're all here." Heath's booming voice brought her attention back to the meeting.

She glanced up, seeing Nesto directly across from her, his gaze locked on hers. Although he said nothing, she could feel the intensity of his stare and shifted uncomfortably in her chair. The smirk on his face irked her.

"Rafe, Jace, and I know you've all been wondering about the secrecy of this meeting." He looked at his brothers, then continued. "There has been much happening over the last weeks, most of it behind closed doors. Today, we're ready to present it all to you. First, however, Jace is going to review some acquisitions of interest to us. We want your initial reactions, but won't be doing a deep dive into them at this meeting." Nodding at Jace, Heath took his seat at the head of the table.

"We have an interest in three potential acquisitions." Jace walked to the cabinet on the wall, sliding back a large panel. Three names were listed, along with their industries.

"You're shitting me." Sean's initial reaction to seeing the name of a large and profitable dude ranch broke the ice, causing several people to laugh.

Jace chuckled, then turned serious. "Not at all. Serenity's dude ranch and tour operations have become the standard for those companies wanting to be at the top of the industry." He looked at Sean. "In case I'm not being clear, that would be us. As you know, MacLaren Enterprises does nothing halfway. Neither does Serenity. Plus, they are as committed to programs for disadvantaged children as we are. In a short time, Sean has established our resort division as a strong competitor to Serenity. Instead of fighting them, we're looking at folding them into our company, which will more than double the resort business. Of course, Sean would most likely oversee the transition and continue to head the division."

"Oh Lord." Sean's good-natured moan brought more snickers, although they all knew he'd put all his efforts into making it happen. He'd also formed an emotional bond with their program, which offered a camp and skill building for children in the foster care system.

"As Heath said, we aren't opening the discussion yet. That will come later." Sliding back another panel, Jace revealed the second company. "Champion Horse Breeding is looking for a buyer."

Kade's eyes went wide. "No shi...uh, kidding."

"Exactly," Rafe offered. "We've been watching them a long time. The founder is in his late eighties with no heirs interested in taking it over. A syndicate of investors is considering a purchase, but they lack the knowledge and depth in the industry."

Jace nodded. "Rafe is right. The timing may be perfect. The fact they have operations in Arizona and Montana is a huge plus for us. Again, we'll table further discussion until later." Glancing at Heath, he revealed the final panel.

"My God," Skye gasped. "Does Gage know about this?" She shot a look at her father, whose expression told her Gage already knew. "That scoundrel. He never said a word to me."

Rafe sent her an understanding look. "Honey, in Gage's defense, we required he keep our discussions to himself. Honestly, he didn't like it one bit. If it makes you feel better, he and Ivan are flying in after lunch to join us. Gage will be staying a few days."

The scowl on Skye's face softened. "In that case, you're all forgiven." With Gage living in Houston and Skye in Crooked Tree, they weren't together as much as they liked. She hoped they'd find a solution before their wedding in a few weeks.

Rafe barked out a quick laugh. "All right, Jace. I believe it's safe to continue."

"I don't know if I need to explain this last one. We've been partners with Double Ace for close to two years. It's been a good partnership, but they'd like to change the agreement. Ivan Santiago, Kade's cousin, has worked out a deal with his father and the other investors to allow us to buy them outright. We'd absorb the business, rebranding it under our name. Because of the issues last year, resulting in threats against our family, they're willing to offer us an incredible deal. However, as with the other two, we'll need to go through the process to make a decision, although we believe this one is almost a given."

Heath stood, closed the panels, then faced those around the table. "Three excellent possibilities to enlarge our holdings. Each one requires thorough due diligence."

"Seems like you're pretty certain about all of them. Do we really need to discuss this further before taking a vote?" Eric asked.

Sean cleared his throat. "Easy for you to say. None of the three fall under real estate and development. Kade's team will have two companies to dig through. At least my team will have just the one."

"You make a good point, Sean." Heath picked up a piece of paper, scanning the contents. "If we decide it's worth continuing our review of all three, everyone in this room will be involved. We'll designate work groups to spread it all out."

"If we go forward, what's the timing for a final decision?" Trey had kept quiet, absorbing the process while listening to other opinions. He knew they might go easy on him for a short time, but he wanted to contribute as soon as possible.

"We generally allow two to four weeks, depending on the size of the acquisition," his father answered. "You'd rotate between all three."

"Throwing me into the fire fast, Dad?"

"Real fast," Heath replied with a broad smile. As the laughter quieted, Heath let out a breath, then glanced at his two brothers, who both nodded. "I know this will be hard, but for a little while, we need you to tuck all of what you've heard away. We'll spend more time on it later, depending on how the next announcement goes."

"You mean there's more?" Sean asked, raising his eyebrows.

Cam chuckled. "You didn't think three simple acquisitions was the reason for all the secrecy, did you, Sean?"

He shrugged, leaning back in his chair. "If anyone can tell me how our fathers operate, I'm all ears."

Mitch's gaze focused on Rafe. "So, Pops, if what you've already told us isn't the big news, what is?"

Heath looked at his brother. "Go ahead, Rafe."

Nodding, Rafe stood, looking at each face. Some showed excitement, others concern. He still didn't know how he felt about it, and neither did his brothers. Rubbing a hand on the back of his neck, he took a deep breath.

"We've received an offer to buy out MacLaren Enterprises."

Chapter Six

Cam dropped the pen he'd been holding. Mitch mumbled a raw curse. Kade, Trey, and most of the others sat in shocked silence. You could hear the whirl of the air conditioning, traffic in the parking lot, and the measured breaths of those around the table.

The first to recover, Cassie looked at Heath. "You turned them down, right, Dad?"

Heath didn't flinch. "No, Cassie, we didn't."

"Must have been a heck of an offer." Eric clicked his pen open, then closed, his voice flat.

"I'm guessing you'll go over the particulars so we can talk about it."

Rafe nodded, walking to a nearby table to pick up a stack of folders. "There's one for each of you. Instead of discussing it now, we're asking you to take a couple hours to have lunch, then return here at one thirty. We'll stay as long as necessary to answer questions and hear all your comments."

Heath and Jace joined Rafe by the door, waiting until everyone had a folder before Heath spoke.

"We know this is a shock and want you to know we haven't made any decision. We'll see all of you in two hours."

"What the hell?" Sean voiced the sentiment they all seemed to be thinking as they opened the folders and began to read.

Matt turned to the offer amount, then blew out a low whistle. "That's a lot of money."

"Yeah," Eric and Brooke answered at the same time.

Standing, Trey stretched his arms above his head, looking at the others. "I know this is my first meeting of this nature, but I suggest we order sandwiches and dig into this monster."

Cam reached behind him to grab a menu from a local sandwich shop. "Heath's assistant can do that for us. She already knows what most of us want. For the rest of you, take a look and give me your order."

Mitch didn't look up from reading the offer. "Whiskey. Straight."

"Make it two." Matt skimmed the rest of the information, then leaned back. "Do you think Annie, Caroline, and Reyna know about this?"

Sean nodded. "I have no doubt the wives know about this. Must have killed them not to say anything at the house yesterday. This is a bombshell."

Skye let out a breath, thinking of her younger sister and brother. "Samantha and Rhett aren't going to like this at all. They've set their sights on being with the company a long time."

Kade tossed down the folder and stood. "I don't know about the rest of you, but I need some air. Brooke? Nesto?"

Brooke stood to join him at the door.

"I'm with you." Nesto looked at Paige. She'd left everything behind to take the new job. Now it might have all been for nothing. "Why don't you join us, Paige?"

She glanced at him, her eyes widening at the offer. "I, um..."

"It's all right. I promise I won't bite." Nesto saw the curious gazes of the others, but didn't care. He needed to start clearing the air with Paige and wanted to start now.

"Sure." She followed him into the hall, heading toward an atrium in the lobby where Kade and Brooke were seated. "Hope you don't mind if I join you."

Brooke cocked a brow when she saw Paige walking next to Nesto. "Of course not. Take a seat so we can shake out this deal together."

"Quite a surprise." Nesto sat back, folding his arms, every nerve in his body attuned to the fact Paige sat a couple feet away.

"Nothing could've surprised me more. Mom didn't say a word." Brooke rested a hand on her growing belly, her thoughts jumbled.

Kade reached over, settling a hand over his wife's. "There's been no decision, but it's a lot of money. The brothers would be fools not to seriously consider it."

Brooke let out a deep breath. "I know. It just came as such a surprise."

"I don't know why." They turned to look at Paige. "Think about it. MacLaren Enterprises is extremely successful, diversified, with excellent management. I'd be surprised if they didn't regularly receive offers on individual divisions or the entire company."

Brooke nodded. "Well, someone wants the entire operation. The proposal mentioned keeping the management team intact, but you know how that goes. We stay for a year, maybe two, then they bring in their own people. I highly doubt they'd keep either one of us, Paige. It's mainly giant companies that include what we do in-house. Most outsource organizational development and merger and acquisition transition programs."

Kade grinned. "You could always stay at home with the baby. It wouldn't hurt you to take some time off."

Nesto and Paige both groaned, already knowing where that comment would lead.

Brooke glared at her husband. "And have *you* ever taken time off from any job? Hmmm, let me think. No, I don't believe you have. What makes you think I want to?"

Holding up his hands, Kade shook his head. "Just a thought, darlin'. The baby will change life for both of us. It wouldn't hurt if one of us didn't work for a while."

Nesto leaned forward, resting his arms on his legs. "This is all speculation, guys. Something tells me it's a test case the brothers are putting in front of everyone to gauge our reaction. The question is, do you want to stay with the company, or will this give you an opportunity to stretch yourself somewhere else?"

"I hate these *expand your horizons* talks. Right now, I just want everything to stay the way it is—at least until a year or two after all the babies arrive. I mean, how many of us are pregnant right now?" Brooke asked, again resting her hand on her stomach.

"At last count, four. Mitch and Dana are talking about starting a family, and it wouldn't surprise me if Eric and Amber are considering it, as well." Kade leaned back in his chair.

"They are," Brooke confirmed. "Eric told me a couple months ago they're ready to have kids. Geez, can you imagine seven or eight little ones running around the ranch house."

Paige laughed. "Lainey already runs the company daycare centers. Might need a new one just for family." Her smile disappeared as a flash of pain rushed through her at seeing the look of regret on Nesto's face.

"Yeah, well...it's something to consider when discussing the offer." Nesto watched the door open, a young man carrying several bags walking inside. "Looks like lunch is here."

Kade stood, holding out a hand to help Brooke up. "Time to get down to business, boys and girls. This is going to be an interesting afternoon."

Paige lagged behind the others as they walked to the conference room, feeling her phone vibrate in her pocket. Instinct told her it was Paul. Still, she had to be certain.

"I'll meet you in there," she said to their backs, believing they hadn't heard her as she pulled the phone from her pocket and walked into a small alcove. Seeing the name, she answered, deciding to put a stop to his calls. "I'm at work."

"Sorry, sis, but it's important we meet when I come to town."

Blowing out a frustrated breath, she turned her back, not seeing Nesto hovering a few feet away.

"I already told you I'm not interested in hearing about your current business ventures. They are your decisions, not mine."

"Come on, Paige. I need your help. Can't you spare me a few minutes?"

Touching two fingers to her temple, she massaged, trying to calm her reaction to what she knew was another illegal scheme by her brother. "Call me tonight and we'll talk. I'm not agreeing to anything until I hear more about it."

"What time?"

"Eight."

"Fine, if that's the best you can do. But don't ignore my call." He hung up, leaving her trembling.

"You all right?"

She jumped at Nesto's voice from right behind her. "Um, yes...fine."

"That didn't sound like it. Was it Paul?"

Her eyes widened for an instant before she calmed her features. "Doesn't matter. I can handle it."

"Yeah, I've heard that before."

Crossing her arms, she glared at him. "What does that mean?"

Scrubbing a hand down his face, Nesto shook his head. "Forget it. They're waiting for us." He didn't wait for her to respond before turning to walk to the conference room.

"Nesto?"

Without stopping, he held up a hand, silencing whatever she'd been about to say, then disappeared through the door.

Dropping her head, Paige let her racing heart calm before following. Plastering a serene look on her face, she stepped inside, taking her seat next to Brooke. She knew they were in for a hectic afternoon and couldn't afford to let Paul's phone call or Nesto's comments bother her.

Opening her folder, she listened as the group went through each page and every detail. From the questions and comments, it seemed clear to Paige no one wanted to approve the deal. The missing piece seemed to be the buyer. They weren't listed and nothing in the offer gave a clue as to their identity.

After an hour, they'd finished their sandwiches, concluding the discussion as Heath, Rafe, and Jace walked back in, taking their seats.

"Enough time?" Heath asked, looking at the serious faces around the table.

"Who's the buyer?" Mitch shoved the folder away, then crossed his arms.

"Takaki Holdings."

"Damn. Aren't they the Japanese firm aggressively buying American companies?" Trey asked.

Heath looked at his son, nodding. "The same. You've heard of them?"

"The wife of one of the pilots in my squadron used to work for them. Bright lady. Has a couple master's degrees and speaks four languages." Trey grimaced. "She always spoke highly about the company."

"Why'd she quit?" Kade asked.

Trey chuckled. "Triplets."

"The offer says most employees would stay with the company." Kade's brows furrowed as he reread a specific page. "But they'd offer no guarantees and no severance after six months. Is that standard?"

"Nothing is standard in these deals. It's all a negotiation." Heath uncapped his bottle of water, taking a long swallow.

Mitch leaned forward, resting his arms on the table, looking at Rafe. "Pops, do you want to sell?"

"It's not my decision."

"That's a horrible non-answer, Pops." Skye shook her head.

Trey tapped his pen on the folder, clearing his throat. "We'd lose control, the ability to expand and do deals the way we want. They could shut down operations or sell them off piece by piece and there'd be nothing we could do."

"I'd be surprised if they continued our support of foster kids or the camp Sean runs. We've worked so hard to keep those programs going, I'd hate to see them shut down."

"Cassie's right. No Japanese firm is going to care about American foster children or the work we do with them." Sean dragged in a breath, shaking his head. "Are we really that desperate for money?"

Rafe answered. "It's not about the money, son. We have to focus on what's best for the company and our employees."

"Well, hell. Then I don't see any reason to continue the discussion." Sean stood, grabbing a bottle of water from the table behind him.

Rafe looked at Heath and Jace, who made no indication as to their thoughts. "How about we do this. Let's go around the table. Everyone vote either yes to continue discussion with Takaki or no to take it off the table. Sound good?"

Everyone nodded.

Rafe looked at Mitch. "Why don't you start?"

"No."

"Sean?"

"Absolutely no."

"Skye?"

"No."

Rafe turned to Heath and Jace. "I'm sensing a pattern here. Let me ask this. Is there anyone at the table who plans to vote *yes*?" No one responded. "No one believes it's worth taking the next step?" They all shook their heads. "Heath?"

Standing, Heath picked up his own folder and held it up. Grabbing it with both hands at the top, he ripped it in half. "Done. Now, let's move on to the three acquisitions."

Paige closed her binder, excited at the turn of events and her role in reviewing the three companies. She was also mentally spent, dreaming of a glass of wine and another long soak in the tub.

"Who's up for drinks and dinner?" Sean strolled down the hall, his enthusiasm contagious.

Paige followed behind Nesto, smiling at the exuberance in Sean's voice.

"Aren't you tired, bro?" Kade glanced at his younger brother, who looked as if he hadn't spent ten hours in meetings.

"Heck no. I'm just getting started. Nesto, you're good for staying out a while, right? Maybe you can hook up with that gorgeous redhead you've been seeing. Val, isn't it?"

Paige's breath caught. It shouldn't surprise her Nesto had found someone else. After all, it had been two years since she left. A man as good-looking and smart as him wouldn't have to look hard for female companionship. Still, it hurt to think of him with someone else.

"I'll let you boys figure out your evening. See you all tomorrow." Pushing past them, Paige walked as fast as possible, not wanting to hear anything more about Nesto's woman.

"Nice, Sean." Kade shook his head, taking Brooke's hand as they walked outside.

Sean cocked his head. "What did I say?"

Nesto watched Paige leave. He hadn't missed the pain on her face at Sean's comment or the way she'd almost run from the building. "No worries. I'm beat, though. See you tomorrow."

"Sure, Nesto. See you tomorrow."

He didn't respond, heading outside to see if he could catch Paige. Searching the parking lot, he saw the empty spot where she'd parked the car Annie loaned her. It shouldn't matter what she thought of him seeing other women. She'd made the decision to end their relationship, not him.

Sliding into his truck, he followed the road to his cabin, more than ready for a cold beer and the chicken enchiladas tucked in the refrigerator. Pulling into the carport, he turned off the engine, seeing Paige slowly walking to her front door. Stopping to insert the key, she glanced over her shoulder, looking straight at him.

A pang of desire, strong enough to suck the air from his lungs, ripped through him. She held his gaze a moment longer before opening her door to disappear inside. He wanted to follow her, force Paige to tell him why she'd left him. Had she met someone else? Or did she simply fall out of love with him? Had he misjudged her feelings for him so completely? He wanted answers to the questions that still burned in his mind.

Climbing out of his truck, he entered the dark cabin, leaving the lights off as he walked to the refrigerator. Pulling out a beer, he chugged it down, slamming the empty bottle on the counter. Ignoring the pangs of hunger, he stripped, leaving his clothes on the floor as he stepped into the shower. The cold prickles of icy water stung, but it was a welcome pain.

He needed to snap himself out of it, stop obsessing over Paige and put her in the past. Getting out of the shower, he wrapped a towel around his waist, then grabbed his phone, doing the only thing he knew to ease the pain.

"Hey, it's Nesto. I know it's late, but if you aren't doing anything, I thought I'd come by."

Ten minutes later, he climbed back into his truck, not sparing a glance at the cabin next door as he headed into town.

Chapter Seven

Paige woke from a restless sleep to the sound of her phone. Before thinking, she grabbed it, putting it to her ear.

"Hello?"

"It's Paul. Did I wake you?"

"Do you have any idea what time it is?" She sat up, drawing the covers over her.

"It's after eight here. That would make it, uh…"

"Just past five in the morning, Paul. Give me a couple more hours, then call back."

"Wait. I really need to talk with you, and you didn't answer my call last night."

Paige grimaced. She had told him to call, but after such a long day, she'd climbed into the tub, forgetting all about it. "All right. Tell me what's going on."

"Thanks, sis. I'll make it brief." She could hear the relief in his voice. "I've been working with an organization out your way and they want to expand distribution. It's a big opportunity for me."

"What does that have to do with me?"

"They want an introduction to the MacLaren family. I know you're tight with them, so I thought you could set something up."

Paige closed her eyes, shaking her head. She was beginning to believe her brother was certifiably nuts. "Not a chance, Paul."

"Hey, I'm not asking for anything except an introduction. You know, one of the head guys. Someone who can make decisions."

"Absolutely not, Paul. They're my friends and my employer. If that's all, I'm hanging up."

"No, wait." The frustration in his voice didn't sway her.

"I'm tired and have several long days ahead of me. You're going to have to find someone else to help you out."

"There *is* no one else, Paige." She could hear him taking a couple deep breaths before he continued. "Look, I'm in trouble. My partners are after me to set up new deals, but I don't have the connections. They've given me a month to make this work or..." His voice trailed off, but not before she heard the fear in his voice. "Please, Paige. If you do this, it will be the last time I ask you for anything."

The instant the words left his mouth, she knew it was a lie. He'd severed all ties with his old friends and alienated his family. Paul didn't have anyone else, but that didn't mean she'd support his illegal actions.

"You ask too much of me. These are good people who've given me a chance at a great company. They trust me, and I refuse to do anything to betray their faith in me." Paige waited for him to explode. Instead, there was a long pause before he finally spoke.

"You're going to wish you'd helped me out."

Before she could respond, the line went dead. Setting the phone aside, she fell back on the bed, covering her eyes with her arm. Her stomach clenched, disgust and fear consuming her. She didn't know any details of Paul's business and didn't want to learn any more than she already knew. And she'd never, ever involve the MacLarens.

The clock told her she had at least two hours before everyone would convene again. She had to do something to calm herself and kill a little time. Opening a drawer, she pulled out her running gear. A few minutes later, she grabbed her key and headed outside, noticing Nesto's truck missing from in front of his cabin. She knew what it meant. Sean had mentioned a redhead Nesto had been seeing. Val, if she remembered correctly. It didn't take much to figure out where he'd gone. Trying not to let it hurt, she took a couple deep breaths, then started jogging away from the cabin.

She'd gone about a quarter mile when a shout drew her attention.

"Hey, Paige. Hold up."

Jogging in place, she smiled when she saw Kade coming up beside her.

"Care for company?"

"Sure." She started off again, Kade running next to her. "It's still dark and I don't know my way around yet."

"Nesto and I run a certain loop all the time. He was supposed to meet me, but he's a no-show."

Paige nodded, not wanting to think about who he was with and what they were doing. It would've been so much easier if she had fallen out of love with him and broke it off. If anything, her love had grown, sometimes making it hard to breathe when she saw him.

"You ready to start reviewing the companies?" She needed to get her mind off Nesto...and Paul. Thinking of either messed with her mind.

"Heck yeah. Three great prospects are on the table. Wouldn't surprise me if we approved all of them."

She glanced at him as they started up an uphill trail. "Does the company have the kind of resources needed to take on all three?"

"Given the numbers I've seen, we could take on at least six that are in the same range as the ones we're reviewing."

"Cash cow, huh?" Brooke, Kade, and Heath had shared some numbers with her on the company, but with MacLaren Enterprises being privately held, there wasn't much more she could find.

"They're shrewd, careful in their investments, and have excellent people in key positions. From my perspective, yes, they do have a good amount of cash on hand for expanding operations."

"Appears I came on at a good time." She couldn't help her excitement at her new role. It felt as if it had been designed for her.

"Everyone has the same goal. At least we do after Heath tore up the proposal from Takaki Holdings."

"I don't think your father or uncles had any intention of going forward. They wanted validation from the rest of you, as well as a confirmation of everyone's commitment."

Kade nodded as they made the turn back toward the cabins. "Well, they got it."

They ran in silence for several minutes before Paige's place came into view, seeing a pair of headlights moving along the road.

"Oh no," she breathed out, not realizing Kade had heard.

Glancing at her, he slowed his pace. "Look, I don't know what happened to make you leave. What I do know is Nesto hasn't gotten over it."

"Yeah...neither have I."

Kade's gaze narrowed on her, understanding hitting him. "What he's doing now is a way for him to cope with you being so close. It's not meant to hurt you."

She let out a breath, watching as Nesto came to a stop and climbed out of the truck. When his eyes locked with hers, she couldn't help but feel a mixture of desire and regret.

"Hey, bro. Did you forget our run?" Kade stopped beside him. It didn't prevent Nesto from continuing to stare at her, his face a mask.

"Yeah. I should've sent you a text."

"Thanks for the run, Kade. Let me know if you want to do it again sometime." Turning, she walked inside her cabin, closing the door on a quiet click.

"Jesus." Nesto continued to watch her door as he shredded a hand through his hair.

"You been with the redhead I heard about?"

"Her name's Val, and yeah," he blew out.

"Serious?"

Nesto's gaze shot to Kade. "No. Nice lady, but...no. A place to be when it all closes in on me."

"Look, it's not my business, so tell me to back off if I'm out of line."

Nesto's gaze narrowed. "Go on."

"I think you and Paige should talk."

"Why? Did she say something?"

Kade put his hands on his hips. "I don't know, man. My gut tells me the two of you aren't over."

Nesto let out a mirthless laugh. "We're through all right. Dead and buried is more like it."

"Believe that if you want. Like I said, it's not my business. I'd better get back home and shower. See you at the office." Kade took off at a slow run, knowing Nesto would chew on what he'd said.

The run had helped Paige clear her mind of the disturbing conversation with Paul. It hadn't helped push images of Nesto with another woman out of her thoughts. She had no right to be jealous or angry. He didn't belong to her anymore, hadn't in over two years, and would never be hers again. Somehow, her heart didn't get the message, even if her brain had.

Paige hadn't considered dating or trying to meet someone else. For months, she'd worked to help her brother. Even without that distraction, she knew there'd never be anyone else for her. As much as she wanted a family, she'd never settle for anyone else. Her heart would always be Nesto's. The knowledge saddened her, leaving a void in her future that would never be filled.

It didn't take long to shower and dress. She wanted to focus on the challenges ahead of her and the limitless opportunities of working with Brooke, not on her own broken state. Nesto had met someone, and he, more than anyone, deserved to be happy. Never again would she interfere with his heart.

Pulling into the parking lot, she grabbed her laptop and purse, then walked into the entry. Sharing greetings with the receptionist, she took the elevator to her office, wanting to review the files once more before everyone met. After thirty minutes, she stood, ready to grab coffee and meet the others.

Brooke walked in, holding out a cup of coffee. "Here you go. Just the way you like it—too much cream and enough sugar to sink a ship."

Paige reached for it, then took a sip. "Hmmm...perfect. I didn't take time to make coffee at home. You're an angel."

"I keep telling Kade that. Not sure it has sunk in yet."

Paige grinned. "That man worships the ground you walk on. Never doubt you're his angel." Picking up her files, she followed Brooke to the conference room.

"Here's the drill. We'll review the files on all three companies, then divide into groups, each tasked with doing a deep dive into one of the targets. Each group will work with legal and finance. You, Nesto, and I will rotate between teams."

Paige bit her lip, nodding.

"I know it sounds complicated, but it's not. We're very informal, so don't worry about stepping on toes. My guess is Heath, Jace, and Rafe will task themselves with overseeing each team. They don't interfere, just make themselves available. If it goes as in the past, we'll meet at four o'clock each afternoon to check progress, make adjustments to the schedule, and confirm our continued interest in each company. Dinner is sometimes brought in so we can work late. Other times, we're cut loose around seven." Brooke looked at Paige as they stopped outside the conference room door. "You ready?"

Paige smiled. "Totally."

She and Brooke took the same two seats as the day before, which meant she'd be staring across the table at Nesto most of the day. No problem. They both had jobs to do, and even if her evenings were spent alone with a glass of wine, she felt an excitement about her future for the first time in months.

"About time you two wandered in." Sean leaned back, crossing his arms, as Skye and Gage took seats across from him. "We had a bet going to see if you'd just head off to Vegas, spare all of us another wedding."

"Not a chance." Gage rested an arm across Skye's shoulders. "It would take a miracle to talk your sister into something so quick and easy."

He and Ivan Santiago had joined the meeting late the day before, just in time for the discussion on MacLaren Enterprises acquiring Double Ace. Afterward, Skye and Gage had disappeared, while Ivan left with Heath and Rafe for supper with Annie and his aunt Reyna, Rafe's wife.

"Are we ready to get started?" Heath walked in, followed by Jace and Rafe.

"Can't wait." Sean's bland tone reflected how much he looked forward to bringing on another dude ranch, even a premier western experience such as Serenity.

"Good. Sean, as I'm sure you expected, you will be the lead on reviewing Serenity."

"Yes, sir."

"Kade, you'll be the lead on Champion Horse Breeding, and Mitch will take on Double Ace. Cameron, Brooke, Paige, and Nesto will form their own work group, which will move between each of the other teams." Heath looked around, raising a brow. "Has anyone seen Nesto this morning?"

Before anyone could answer, the door opened, Nesto walking in to take the only empty chair—across from Paige, the same as the day before. He spared her a quick glance, then leaned over to whisper something to Kade.

"Nesto. Glad you could join us." Heath gave him a pointed look.

"Sorry, sir."

"I just finished telling everyone you, Cameron, Brooke, and Paige will be forming your own group since you'll be reviewing all team proposals. Any problem with that?"

Glancing at Paige, he turned back to Heath. "No, sir."

"Glad to hear it." Heath looked around the table. "The binders in front of you contain the team you'll be on and the process we use for reviewing potential acquisitions. Use it. As you work through it, remember no question or comment is stupid. Don't feel anything is off limits. We want final recommendations within fourteen days. Questions?" When no one commented, he smiled. "Then let's get started."

By seven o'clock, Jace stopped everyone, telling them to head home. The day had gone well, Nesto treating her with respect, asking her thoughts, giving his opinions. She did her best to do the same, even as her thoughts wandered to the image of his messed hair and rumpled clothes when she'd seen him pull up to his cabin that morning.

"Well, I'm bushed. Stopping for Chinese, then home and bed." Paige stood, picking up her purse and laptop. "See you all in the morning."

"Wait up, Paige. I'll walk out with you." Nesto nodded to the others, not sure why he'd asked her to wait. Joining her in the hall, he kept a good amount of distance between them.

"I don't need an escort. I'd think you'd have somewhere to be."

He lifted a brow. "Such as?"

"The redhead Sean mentioned. Isn't that who you were with last night?" She stopped, then leaned against the wall, shaking her head. "I'm sorry. It's none of my business who you see." Swallowing the bile in her throat, she pushed away from the wall. "It would be best if I walked out alone." She hurried away, bypassing the elevator in favor of the stairs.

"Slow up or you'll fall." Nesto moved beside her with natural grace, one of the many traits that had drawn her to him. He cupped her elbow, remembering how her balance sometimes betrayed her. At the bottom, she moved away.

"Thanks. I'll see you tomorrow."

"We're halfway to your car already. Don't be stubborn and force me to walk two paces behind you."

She would've laughed if it hadn't been so painful to recall the old joke they once shared.

"Fine." Reaching her car, she pulled out her keys, feeling her phone vibrate in her pocket. "I'd better get this. Thanks for escorting me out."

He nodded, releasing a breath. "Anytime."

Turning away, she didn't recognize the number, but at least it wasn't her brother. "Hello?"

"Is this Paige Wallace?" The voice had a hard edge and thick accent, reminiscent of those she heard in Tijuana on a couple trips into Baja.

"Yes. What can I do for you?"

"Ah, now that sounds promising. Your brother said you wouldn't be cooperative."

Paige froze, glanced at the phone, then turned her head to look for Nesto. Relief flooded her when she saw him only a few feet away, arms folded, watching her. At the look on her face, he moved closer.

"What does this have to do with Paul?"

Put it on speaker, Nesto mouthed when he got within a foot of her. She nodded, touching the icon.

"I see we already have trust issues, Miss Wallace. For a moment, I thought we could have a private conversation. How are you, Marshal Salgado?"

Recognizing the voice, Nesto pushed Paige against her car, shielding her with his body as he looked around, reaching for the gun in his shoulder holster.

"Javé Cruz. What the hell are you doing calling my..." He hesitated, his jaw tightening.

"Your *woman*, Marshal Salgado? I had heard she was no longer in your life. It seems I am wrong. Miss Wallace, we will have to find another time to talk. Alone. Have a pleasant evening."

The call ended, Paige dumbstruck at the brief conversation. Blinking a couple times, she focused on Nesto, seeing the anger and confusion in his eyes.

His nostrils flaring, he grasped her arm, turning to face her. "Do you want to tell me what the hell that was about?"

She forced down the fear in her gut, shaking her head, her body beginning to tremble. "I don't know who that was or what he wants."

"Well, he sure knows you. And Paul. In my opinion, that's not a good sign."

Her pale face and scared eyes looked up at him. "Who is he, Nesto?"

Raking a hand through his hair, he blew out a breath. "Javé Cruz, president of the Devil's Sons motorcycle club. He's a murderer, partner with the Montalvo-Ortiz cartel...and he's watching."

Chapter Eight

Paige sat in the living room of Nesto's cabin, her shaky hands gripping a glass of whiskey. Before meeting Nesto, she'd never tried it. When stressed, it had become her drink of choice.

Nesto paced back and forth in front of her before taking a seat in his oversized leather chair. His face had taken on the blank expression she'd seen many times when given a difficult assignment. This time, his brows furrowed when he looked at her. Leaning forward, he rested his arms on his legs, clasping his hands together.

"Start from the beginning. I need to know what led up to the call from Javé."

Taking a sip of whiskey, she hesitated, not knowing where to start. Nesto no longer worked as a federal marshal, but he still kept strong ties with the agency. This time, however, she didn't believe what she told him could damage him in any way. Still, after all these months of not confiding in him, she hesitated.

"I can see your mind is in full gear, trying to figure out what to say and what to leave out. I'm warning you, Paige. There's no room for anything except the complete story. Tell me everything—now."

Staring at the contents in her glass, allowing it to be her focal point, she started from the beginning with the first call from her father. She spoke of how she'd turned down his request for help with Paul, telling him it was his turn to figure out what to do with his wayward son. Then Peter Wallace had pulled out all the stops and gone with the one thing he knew Paige couldn't refuse—her mother's pleading request.

From there, the story flowed quickly, detailing Paul's latest phone calls, ending with tonight. All the while, Nesto stayed still, his hard gaze boring into hers, looking for any sign of dishonesty. His expression never changed. It had been hard as granite when she started recounting the story that had altered both their lives, and ended with the same cold detachment.

"As far as you know, are the labs still on your parents' properties?"

She glanced up and nodded. "Yes."

"And you're certain they're meth labs?"

"I never saw them, Nesto. My father is the one who went through one of them when no one was around. He's certain it's meth."

"Did they take out a restraining order on Paul to keep him off their land?"

"I don't believe so. At least my father never mentioned it."

"Is there any proof at all the labs belong to Paul?"

A confused expression crossed her face. "Who else could they belong to?"

The first sign of frustration sounded in Nesto's voice. "Your father never asked Paul outright if they were his?"

"I overheard him talking to Paul on the phone once, telling him he had to close them down. According to my father, Paul didn't deny they were his. I don't believe he ever came right out and said they belonged to him, but he did say he couldn't close them down."

Standing, Nesto paced to the window, shoving his hands into his pockets. He didn't turn toward her when he spoke. "Paul said he had business out here and wanted to meet with you, correct?"

"As I said, he called more than once. On the last call, he asked for me to make introductions. His *business partner* wanted to talk with someone high up in MacLaren Enterprises. Someone who could make decisions."

This time, Nesto turned to stare at her. "Paul didn't mention the topic of discussion?"

"No. He said his business partners were giving him a month to come up with new deals, but he never mentioned what the deals were about. Except..." Her voice trailed off as she tried to recall Paul's exact words.

"Except?"

"Each time he called, Paul intimated his businesses dealings were legal."

Nesto snorted. "And you believed him?"

Taking another swallow of whiskey, she set the glass down and stood, anger creeping into her voice. "No, I didn't believe him. I haven't believed him in a long time. Even though he pleaded, I refused to help him. Enough of my life has been ruined because of Paul and his actions."

Nesto knew she didn't mean just the messes she'd helped him out of or the money he'd been given in the hope of aiding him. The moisture glistening in her eyes told him Paul had ruined her life in other ways, including pushing her to break off her relationship with Nesto. Not even the knowledge she'd done it to keep him out of trouble cracked his anger or the reality she hadn't trusted him with the truth. In Nesto's world, omitting the truth ranked right up there with lying.

He shoved aside any feelings of sympathy for her. She'd been the one to make the choice to keep the truth from him. Nesto would do what he could to keep her and the MacLarens safe, but that didn't mean anything had changed between them.

If anything, the reasons she gave for trying to shield him created a more intense burning rage than when she'd given him no reason at all. If anyone could have helped Paige and her family, it would've been Nesto. He couldn't get beyond the fact she didn't trust him enough to confide in him.

"What do you think this Javé guy wants? Maybe if I meet with him, explain there's nothing I can do—"

"Absolutely not, Paige. I'm not certain of the next steps, but you are not going to meet with Javé or any of his officers. Ever."

Pulling out his phone, Nesto punched in a number. "Hey, bro. I have a situation. When can you be at my cabin?"

Paige stared at him as he fixed them something to eat. The Chinese food she'd planned had been forgotten, along with her appetite, until Nesto mentioned eating. That's when her stomach perked up.

He'd changed over the last couple years. The close-cropped, military haircut had been replaced with longer hair, almost touching his collar. The slight wave of his dark, silky strands held a hint of red under the kitchen lights. His handsome face still had a hard edge, the dark stubble on his jaw and chin giving him a dangerous look, warning off those who considered confronting him. At almost six feet tall, he wasn't as tall as most of the MacLarens, yet his broad shoulders and muscled arms underscored the fact he could hold his own. Of course, anyone who knew of Nesto's Special Forces background would already be aware of his abilities.

Paige had often wondered how a warrior such as Nesto had found a doctoral student so intriguing. Especially one who'd grown up with everything, never wanting for the basics, such as food and shelter. Nesto had struggled every day of his life, worked hard to achieve success, and never wavered from his strong values and bond with Kade.

She and Brooke, both with blonde hair, fair skin, and blue eyes, used to joke how much they looked alike. When he'd first met Paige, Kade had even asked if they were sisters. In many ways, Nesto and Kade could pass for brothers with their dark good looks and rugged appearance. At one point, Paige wondered if Nesto found her attractive because she was so much like his best friend's girl. Over time, she realized that wasn't the case. Nesto was his own man, making his choices separate from the person he admired beyond all others.

A knock drew her attention to the front door. Pushing it open, Kade stepped inside, his hand gripping Brooke's. Both glanced at Paige, then over at Nesto, before Brooke moved to sit next to her.

"Hey. I didn't know you'd be here."

Paige gave her a small smile. "I didn't expect to be here, either."

Kade's curious gaze moved from Paige to Nesto, who leaned against the kitchen counter, his arms crossed. He hadn't said a word since they walked in, his eyes never leaving Paige.

"What's going on?" Kade opened the refrigerator and pulled out a bottle of water for himself and one for Brooke, carrying it to his wife.

"It's a long, complicated story. I need you to listen and provide your sage advice."

"Sure. Whatever you need."

An hour later, Paige's head felt as if it would split open if Kade or Nesto asked one more question. She'd downed two bottles of water and an aspirin while talking through the entire ordeal a second time, her eyes beginning to cross from shifting between the two men. Rubbing her temples, she looked at Nesto.

"I hope there isn't much else because I'm beat."

Brooke stood, looking at Kade. "Why don't I walk Paige back to her place while you two mull things over?"

"No," both Kade and Nesto answered.

Kade sighed. "Sorry, babe. Until we know what Javé is up to, it's too dangerous for you to be out alone at night." Kade looked at Paige. "Especially for you. Javé has you in his sights, and I'm telling you, that's a dangerous place to be."

"Look, I know some pretty awful stuff involving a motorcycle gang went on before Eric and Amber got married. As I recall, the MacLarens were involved and it got real messy." Paige shot a quick look at Brooke before continuing. "She didn't fill me in on all the details, but I'm trying to understand how what is happening now could be related to the actions of a few years ago."

"Come over here and we'll lay it out for you." Nesto pulled out a chair for Paige at the dining table, then waited until Brooke and Kade sat down. Taking a sheet of paper from the bookcase, he laid it in the center of the table and began to draw boxes, labeling them as he explained.

"When Kade went undercover as a DEA agent, he infiltrated Satan's Brethren motorcycle gang, or *club*, as they prefer to be called. They're a nasty bunch who earn their money trading in guns, drugs, and porn, with a few legit businesses mixed in, such as bike repair shops, part shops, tattoo parlors, and adult entertainment."

"Titty bars," Kade clarified.

Nesto nodded. "Right. Their president is Robbie Morgan." He labeled one box with Satan's Brethren. "Devil's Sons is another outlaw biker gang. They deal in guns, drugs, and women, but they also deal in human trafficking. Selling girls and boys through online auctions to buyers around the world, but mainly to men with money in Central and South America. They are a support club to Satan's Brethren." He labeled another box with Devil's Sons. "Their president is Javé Cruz."

Kade took the pencil from Nesto. "We know Javé has relatives in the Montalvo-Ortiz cartel."

Brooke gasped. "The same cartel suspected of kidnapping Reyna and Ivan's mother?"

"The same," Kade answered. "Brutal people who aren't above anything illegal in order to enrich the cartel." He wrote Montalvo-Ortiz cartel in a third box. "Ivan's uncles, Octavio and Stefan, are suspected of being high up in the organization. We don't know about Ivan's father, Javier. He says he has no cartel connections, but..." He shrugged one shoulder.

Nesto continued. "From the meetings this week, we know Javier has passed along his ownership in Double

Ace to Ivan, as have Octavio and Stefan. This was one of the deals they made with the DEA after the Houston incident a few months back, and is what cleared the company for MacLaren Enterprises to buy it." He took the pencil from Kade, writing Double Ace inside a box. "It doesn't mean the cartel is through with them. Purchasing Double Ace might actually make them a more lucrative target for cartel needs. Expanded capacity, more distribution routes, and better networks."

Paige shook her head. "I'm sorry. I still don't get the connection with Paul or me."

"Bear with us, sweet...uh, Paige." Nesto grimaced at the slip, then went on. "Paul is cooking meth on your parents' land. I'm thinking he has a partner in Devil's Sons. Don't ask me how that happened, but my instincts tell me it did. They buy his meth and distribute it through channels provided by the cartel. The cartel wants two things—revenge on the MacLarens for what happened in Houston, and the ability to extend their reach using company subsidiaries to run their *merchandise*. You, Paige, have been chosen as the person to lay the groundwork."

She shook her head. "Why would I do that?"

Nesto cocked his head. "Because Javé will kill Paul if you don't."

Placing a hand over her mouth, she doubled over. "Excuse me." No one blamed her for hurrying to the bathroom and closing the door.

When Brooke stood to go help her, Nesto placed a hand on her shoulder. "She'll be fine. It's time Paige got an understanding of how low her brother has fallen."

"And how useless her attempts to protect him have become," Kade added, seeing his wife's face darken.

Brooke's eyes flared as indignation raced through her. "She did what any sister would. It's what *you* would do for Skye or Samantha, or any of the MacLarens or Sinclairs, and you know it. Paige loves her brother, but she sees his faults." Brooke looked at Nesto, her eyes soft with understanding. "She didn't make a good decision when she chose to help Paul and leave you behind, but it wasn't done because she didn't love you. She made the hard choice because she *did* love you."

Nesto glanced away, settling his hands on his hips as he shook his head. "She made her choice and it damn sure wasn't me." He let out a breath. "Let's just get on with what we need to do."

Brooke nodded, then leaned forward, reading the boxes again. "Do you think both motorcycle gangs are involved?" She directed her question to Kade.

"We know Devil's Sons are because of Javé. My guess is they're running this outside their association with Satan's Brethren. From what I hear, Robbie's been moving his club further away from illegitimate activities and expanding legitimate ones. I can reach out to a few of my buddies who still work for the DEA and find out what they know."

They looked up as Paige returned and sat down. "Sorry."

"Honey, you know you don't have to apologize. Right, Nesto?" Brooke looked up at him, her gaze penetrating.

"Sure. No apology needed, Paige." His slight scowl, however, told her more than his words.

Clasping her hands tight in her lap, she straightened her back, doing the best she could to present a brave front. "What did I miss after Nesto said Javé might kill Paul?"

Nesto grimaced. It had been an insensitive statement. One he never would have made if the woman sitting near him hadn't been Paige.

"Kade is going to talk to his contacts at the DEA to find out what they're willing to share about Satan's Brethren and Devil's Sons." Nesto looked at him. "You might want to talk with Thad Montgomery, too."

"I'll do that. Nesto and I will meet with the brothers as early as possible tomorrow morning. Even if we don't know the specifics of what Javé and Paul want from you, they need to be on guard and start considering extra security for everyone until this blows over."

Brooke touched his arm. "What if it *doesn't* blow over, Kade?"

Wrapping an arm around her shoulders, he drew her to him. "Darlin', this is just another blip in the life of the MacLarens. It will blow over and the family will be protected."

"I should leave."

Three sets of eyes shifted to Paige—two filled with concern, one with enough contempt to trigger anger.

Nesto crossed his arms, shaking his head. "You don't deal with problems by running away, Paige. I would've thought you might have learned that by now."

Jumping to her feet, she placed her hands on his chest and shoved. "I am *not* running. I'm trying to do what's best for you and everyone else. I don't care if you get it or not." Paige shifted toward Brooke. "If I leave, I'll have no ability to make introductions or be a pawn in their game. The threat to everyone will be eliminated."

Kade shook his head, his expression filled with compassion. "It doesn't work that way. The threat to Paul will still be there for Javé to capitalize on. And now that he believes you and Nesto are still together, I'd bet a month's salary Javé will threaten Nesto, as well."

"Let him threaten me. I don't give a damn what he thinks he can do. I'm more concerned about what will happen to everyone else." Nesto moved to the refrigerator, taking out four more bottles of water and passing them around. "I'd offer something stronger, but I'm afraid we'd all crash."

Chugging down half the bottle, Kade held out his hand to Brooke, helping her stand. "Nesto's right. It's time to get you home. Tomorrow's going to come real quick." They walked to the door before Kade turned, giving Paige a serious expression. "You're staying with Nesto until the threat is over."

Her eyes widened. "What? No. Absolutely not." She shook her head, moving toward the door. "I'll be safe in my own cabin."

"Sorry, honey, but the issue is settled and you didn't get a vote. You may think you'll be safe, but Nesto and I have dealt with these people before. When you're in their sights, you're in serious danger." Kade tightened his arm around Brooke when she started to speak, knowing what she was going to say. "I can't have you at our place, either. Javé knows me, so Brooke and I are already in danger. And, in all honesty, if anything happens, my first priorities will be Brooke and the baby. You need to be with someone whose only concern is you."

"Right. The same man who wishes I'd never returned," she mumbled.

Kade's eyes crinkled at the corners, but he held off a smile. "Nesto would never let anything happen to you, Paige. He'd guard you with his life."

She ignored the knot in her stomach. "I don't want anyone protecting me with their life. I'd rather it be focused on me."

Nesto stilled at her words, casting a quick glance at Kade and Brooke before stepping next to Paige. "It's not a big deal. I have an extra bedroom. Sharing the bath isn't an issue. We've done it before. You'll have full charge of the kitchen."

"Great. We all know you're the better cook."

The corners of Nesto's mouth curved upward. "True. This will give you a chance to knock me off the throne."

He grasped her shoulders, turning her to face him. When she didn't look up, he lifted her chin with his hand. "Stay here. I'll keep you safe while staying out of your way. If you refuse, I'll plant myself outside your cabin."

She let out a breath, eyes full of pain, her words a mere whisper. "You already hate me. This will only make it worse."

His throat worked, a muscle in his jaw twitching as he met her gaze. "I don't hate you, Paige." Taking a step away, he lifted his chin at Kade. "Take your wife home. We'll be fine here."

Kade nodded. "Brooke and I will be here at seven to follow you two in. We'll keep close until this is over."

Paige wandered toward the sofa as Nesto watched them get into Kade's truck and drive away. Turning, he studied her as she tried to find calm in a chaotic situation.

"Let's go get what you need, then hit the sack. You're exhausted, and I'm right there with you."

Nodding, she moved up to him, waiting until he walked outside, then motioned her to join him. Before they stepped off his porch, she turned to him.

"I realize how hard this must be for you, so...thank you."

Chapter Nine

Heath, Rafe, and Jace didn't interrupt as Nesto explained what happened the night before, as well as his and Kade's thoughts. At a little after seven, they'd been fortunate to find all three brothers in their offices and available.

"Kade will be calling his contacts at the DEA, as well as Thad Montgomery. I'll be doing the same on my end with the Marshals Service, but doubt they'll know much. I'm recommending we go back on high alert status at all operations. I've already contacted the company we used when we hired additional bodyguards before and told them to be on standby."

Rafe slapped both hands on the table. "Sonofabitch. I'd hoped we were done with this mess." He looked at Heath. "Has Ivan flown out?"

"No. He and Gage planned to stay through today before flying back to Houston." Heath glanced at Kade. "Should we keep them here a few more days?"

"I'd recommend it. At least until Nesto and I have learned what we can about the current state of Satan's Brethren and Devil's Sons. The DEA used to have someone inside the Sons, but I heard he got made and they pulled him out. It's doubtful they have a man in the Brethren. After my undercover work in the club, Robbie is extra careful about bringing in new prospects."

Jace rested his arms on the table, focusing on Nesto. "Who is the most vulnerable?"

He knew what Jace asked. "Paige, Kade, Brooke, and myself. It's anyone's guess after that. If Javé and the cartel are to have any success, they'll resort to blackmail, threats against our families. The good news is Kade's and Brooke's families are here where we can provide protection. Paige is certain she can get her mother to come out for a visit. Her father is leaving for Europe on a long business trip, which is good timing for us." Nesto shrugged. "In all ways that matter, my family is also here." Everyone knew he thought of the MacLarens and Sinclairs as his family. "Paul is the only one out there."

"How can we be certain Paul and Javé are connected?" Heath stood, pacing to the window to look out on a clear Arizona sky.

"He'll call Paige again." The muscle in Nesto's jaw ticked, his voice turning cold. "He has no choice. She's pretty certain if she asks, he'll confirm his connection with the Sons. If not, Kade and I will find a way to do it."

"If he is, the boy made his own choice by aligning himself with the wrong people. We can't spend resources protecting him when he's the one putting the rest of us in danger."

"I agree with you, Heath." Rafe drummed his fingers on the table as his mind raced through the options. "Four women are expecting. If the Sons or the cartel find out, they'll become a very desirable target."

Kade moved to sit next to him. "You're right, Pops. Brooke, Jesse, and Lainey live on the ranch. Cassie will have to move back here until this is under control. She reports to me, so I can talk to her and Matt."

"She's my daughter. I want to be there when you tell them."

"Sure, Heath. Whatever you want."

"How do we handle the due diligence on the three companies?" Jace asked.

Heath paced back to his chair and sat down. "No change. We keep everyone here at headquarters. If we need to meet with executives from the other companies, we fly them in."

"We need to inform them about what's going on."

Heath looked at the time, then back at Nesto. "The meeting starts in ten minutes. You and Kade will give them the same information you provided us. I don't expect any problems. They already know the drill."

"I'd suggest we put off saying anything until I speak with my contacts at the DEA." Kade pulled out his phone. "Let me get on it, then I'll bring you up to speed before we tell everyone what's going on."

Heath nodded. "Agreed. In the meantime, Nesto, order up additional guards around the ranch and headquarters, as well as bodyguards for Cassie, Jesse, Brooke, Lainey, and Paige."

Rafe shook his head. "You know those ladies aren't going to like it."

Heath snorted. "Ask me if I give a damn."

"I thought my eyes were deceiving me when I saw your name on the phone, Kade. How are you, buddy?" Clive Nelson leaned back in his chair, resting his booted feet on his desk.

"I'm doing fine. Better than I deserve given my history."

"Your history is nothing to be ashamed of, Kade. Wish we could have you back. Hey, that's not why you called, is it?"

Kade laughed, picturing the lanky, unflappable Texan. "Afraid not. Do you have a minute?"

At the question, Clive dropped his feet to the floor and leaned forward. "I'm all ears."

"We have a possible situation involving Satan's Brethren and Devil's Sons. The Montalvo-Ortiz and de la Garza cartels may also be involved. Do you have any intel you can give me?"

"Ooo-wee, buddy. You aren't messing around. Seems you have more enemies now than when you were with the agency." Clive leaned over his desk, glanced around, then lowered his voice. "I've got a shitload of data on all four groups. You'll have to be more specific so I can figure out how I can help you."

Kade spent the next ten minutes outlining what had taken place. "Does anything I've said push your buttons?"

"Possibly. Where are you?"

"Arizona. Why?"

"It just so happens I'm due for a little time off and Arizona sounds real good. You got a place I can stay?"

"As long as you need, Clive. When can I expect you?"

"With any luck, later this afternoon."

Paige forced herself to concentrate as she reviewed the data on each company. It didn't take much effort to see how easy Double Ace would fit into the MacLaren Enterprises strategic plan. Champion Horse Breeding had a more complicated organization and would take more time to evaluate. In her opinion, Serenity would require the longest review. The company consisted of several properties in different states, equipment, livestock, on-site veterinary services, daycare at some locations, and restaurants at all.

Glancing out the window, she thought of the night before, regretting the fact she'd gotten less than three hours of sleep. The look on Nesto's face when he emerged from his bedroom told her he hadn't gotten much more.

She found herself wondering how much the current situation would impact his relationship with the redhead, then mentally slapped herself for wasting time on such a trivial subject. They were facing real danger from the motorcycle clubs and cartels. Worrying about who he slept with shouldn't cause her heart to ache or her eyes to pool with unshed tears. All she had to do was get through a few more days and she'd be back in her own cabin, Nesto continuing the life he'd built without her.

Checking the time, she began gathering the files, looking up when her door opened. Nesto leaned against the doorframe, folders tucked under one arm.

"Did you find out anything?"

"Not as much as we'll learn by the end of today. I'll share what Kade and I came up with at the meeting." Moving so she could walk past, he strolled behind her to the conference room, wishing circumstances were different.

He'd slept little the night before, worries about Paige and the MacLarens controlling his thoughts. The fact she slept in the bedroom next to his didn't help.

She'd taken a shower, emerging from the bath wrapped in a lightweight robe, leaving little to his imagination. Nesto didn't need his imagination to know what was concealed under the thin fabric. He'd seen it, tasted it hundreds of times over the years they were a couple, and still dreamed of being with her again, even as his brain warned him away. Any thoughts of a future with her were misplaced, the same as the list of Christmas items he'd wished for as a kid.

She'd tried to protect him by walking away. Although he understood her reasoning, he couldn't forgive the fact she'd cut him out of the decision, hadn't even considered trusting him. His job with the Marshals Service wouldn't have precluded him from advising her and her parents. If he had all the facts to guide him, it wouldn't have jeopardized his job—not in the way she imagined.

As they reached the conference room, Paige's phone rang, causing them to make eye contact.

"Is it Paul?" Nesto asked.

Checking the number, she nodded, a brow lifting.

"You don't have time for a discussion with him right now. Wait and listen to his voice message."

"What if he's in danger and needs me?"

Taking her by the arm, Nesto lead her into an empty office and closed the door. "Paul does *not* need you Paige. He plans to put you in danger to save himself. You've got to stop playing his protector and see him for the man he's become, not the boy you remember."

"But he's my brother, and you said they might kill him. He's probably scared."

Nesto pushed away his frustration, doing his best to put himself in her place. "No doubt he is, but he put himself in this position, and now wants to drag you into it. I can't let that happen. Can you understand that?"

Drawing in a shaky breath, Paige nodded.

"Javé contacted you last night, but made no threats. He isn't going to do anything until the two of you speak. Hurting your brother now serves him no purpose."

As they spoke, her phone buzzed, indicating she'd gotten a new message. Opening her voicemail, she put the phone on speaker.

"Paige, it's Paul. I'm getting on an airplane and will arrive in Phoenix later this afternoon. Look, I'm sorry to bring you into this, but I have no choice. You need to know a man named Javé Cruz may call you. Don't agree to anything until we talk. Gotta run."

"Sonofabitch," Nesto growled. "Paul is the one who gave Javé your number and location." He grasped Paige by the shoulders. "Do not agree to meet with Paul unless I'm with you. You are *not* to be alone with him, no matter how much he begs. Am I clear?"

Biting her lower lip, Paige glanced away, her mind in turmoil.

Nesto tried another approach. "It isn't just you who is in danger, Paige. Javé won't have any problem going after any of the MacLarens to get what he wants. If he has you, his leverage increases."

Sighing, she slipped her phone into her pocket. "You're right. I'll let you know when I talk to Paul."

"And you won't see him without me."

Letting out a frustrated breath, she nodded. "Fine."

His face softened. "Good. Now, we'd better get into the meeting."

"Well, that isn't what I expected to discuss this morning." Cassie walked out the door with Paige, Brooke, and Amber as they left for lunch. Heath had given them a ninety-minute break after four hours of intense discussions on the current situation. "At least we're all in Fire Mountain."

"We're fortunate we can work from just about anywhere." Brooke looked at Paige. "When will you call your mother?"

"During lunch. The sooner she gets on MacLaren land, the better I'll feel." Glancing behind her, she scowled at the sight of Nesto, Kade, Eric, Sean, and Matt following a few feet behind. "What are they up to?"

A wry grin appeared on Cassie's face. "You didn't think they'd let us go to lunch alone after what's happened, did you? There goes Cam." She nodded toward the walkway leading to a small, quaint structure a hundred yards away. "He's going to check on Lainey at the company daycare. Trey is heading to the ranch to make sure Jesse and Annie are all right. Mitch is going to get Dana and explain what's going on. Until this is over, don't expect any privacy or to go anywhere without one of the men tagging along."

"Paige?" Stopping at her car, she saw Nesto jog up next to her, holding out his hand. "Sean and I are riding with you. The others are going in the company SUV."

Glancing at his outstretched hand, she shook her head. "I can drive."

"Of course you can, but you aren't going to. I'll be able to spot anyone following. If I do, I'll need you and Sean to get license plates and details about occupants."

"Unless they're shooting at us," Sean said as he looked around the lot.

"I doubt they'd take the risk at this point. Right now, they want to know who they're up against. Kade and I want them to know anything they plan won't be easy. Come on, Paige. Hand me the keys."

"Might as well hand them over. We're wasting precious lunch time, as well as an opportunity for me to scope out the lovely waitresses at the restaurant." Sean lifted his brows, drawing a chuckle from Paige and Nesto.

She slapped the keys into the palm of Nesto's hand. "You are not going to be on my heels twenty-four-seven. It just isn't going to happen."

Unlocking the car, he pulled the door open, choosing to ignore the comment, which was wishful thinking on her part. "Slide in. I'm hungry."

Paige ate a few small bites of her sandwich, unable to coerce anything more down her throat. Even with the threat, Cassie and Brooke cleaned their plates. She suspected being pregnant had a lot to do with it. Pushing back from the table, she stood, seeing the scowl on Nesto's face.

"I'm going to the ladies' room. Is that all right?" Sarcasm slipped into her voice, even as she did her best to tamp it down.

"Sure. Just keep vigilant."

Grabbing her purse, she followed the signs down the hall and behind the kitchen to the restrooms in back, seeing no one. Turning the knob, she felt herself being jerked from behind, a hand over her mouth, stifling her scream.

"Javé wants to meet with you." The whispered voice had a slight accent similar to Javé's. Shaking her head, she tried to tear herself from his grasp, stopping when another man stepped around the corner. "No more struggling. Javé has no intention of hurting you. This won't take long."

Glancing behind her, she felt a rush of relief when she saw no sign of Nesto. They'd only hurt him if he tried to intervene. Nodding, she let herself be led out the door, around another building, to a group of motorcycles parked behind a liquor store. On one sat a heavyset man with a bushy mustache, short black hair, and a vest with the word *President* stitched on one side.

"Here she is." Her captor shoved her forward, almost pushing her into the man she believed to be Javé.

"Miss Wallace. It's a pleasure to meet you."

Glaring at him, she straightened her back. "I wish I could say the same, Mr. Cruz."

He chuckled, then his face hardened, the niceties forgotten. "Paul works for me. I want you to do the same."

"That isn't possible."

"I'm afraid it is. Paul is bright, but also very stupid. He didn't know the rules when he became my business partner. From what he says, you are equally as smart. Let's hope that is true. If not, I will have to resort to actions I'm sure you'll find...repulsive."

Paige could feel her hands sweating. Holding her ground, she shook her head. "I doubt you're a fool, Mr. Cruz. However, threatening me, or those I care about, would be a ridiculously foolish action. I have no power over the MacLarens and no sway in their business dealings." She took a breath, noting the amusement on the man's face. "Now, if you'll excuse me..." Turning to leave, she smacked into the solid chest of the man who'd brought her to Javé. When he didn't move, she attempted to step around him, only to be yanked back to face his boss.

"You are brave, but not very wise, the same as your brother. It will be the death of Paul, and possibly you." Javé paused a moment, lifting his chin to the men around them. An instant later, they all sat on their bikes, engines humming. "You think about what I said. I'll get a message to you within a few days."

She held her ground as the bikes roared down a back alley a few seconds before Nesto and Kade ran toward her, guns drawn. Stopping in front of her, Nesto slid the gun into his shoulder holster, running his hands down her arms.

"Are you all right?"

Nodding, she gulped in air. "It was Javé."

"I heard the bikes, but didn't get a good look at anyone." On instinct, he settled an arm around her shoulders, drawing her close. Even with his solid body next to hers, Paige began to shake.

"Two of his men took me out the back. Javé said he'll contact me with what he wants."

The panic in her eyes rocked him. It was all he could do to not kiss her fear away. "He isn't going to get to you again, Paige. Let's get back safe inside the office. You can tell Kade and me everything he said."

Nodding, she let him lead her to the car. Now she had a face to put with the name. Unfortunately, it gave her no comfort at all.

Chapter Ten

Clive Nelson eased his tall frame out of the truck he'd driven from San Diego. The drive relaxed him, allowing time to go over what he'd learned from Kade and what he had to share. Listening to the constant thrumming of country music on the radio, he made good time, arriving at the ranch well before dark. Looking at the front door, he walked forward at the sight of a beautiful, middle-aged woman, blonde hair pulled back into a ponytail.

"Mrs. MacLaren. It's good to see you again." He reached out his hand, surprised when she ignored it in favor of a hug.

"It's good to see you, Clive. Kade told us you'd arrive sometime today." Annie stepped back, studying his face. "Looks like you need a vacation, not another assignment."

He choked out a laugh. "Officially, I *am* on vacation, ma'am."

"You'll be staying with Heath and me. His brother, Rafe, and wife, Reyna, live here, as well. So, please, feel free to call me Annie. Can I help with your bags?"

He cocked his head, his mouth curving into a smile. "No, ma'...uh, Annie. I think I can manage." Pulling them from the back seat, he followed her inside. "Rafe is Kade's father, right?"

"Right. Reyna is his mother." She glanced over her shoulder, looking for a reaction before starting up the stairs to the second floor.

"Geez, I forgot all about that. Well, glad they got back together. I'm sure Kade's happy about it." He followed her to a bedroom right at the top.

"You'll be in here. I'd let you have one of the cabins, but they're all full right now. Unless Kade and Brooke—" She stopped when Clive held up a hand.

"This will do fine. I don't know how long I'll be around. With luck, a few days, then I'll take a side trip to the Grand Canyon, maybe end up in Vegas for a couple days."

The sound of boots on the stairs had them turning to see Kade. "Clive, buddy. Glad to see you made it." They clasped hands, slapping each other's backs.

Annie watched, then turned to leave. "I'll be downstairs if you need anything. Dinner is at seven."

"Is it okay if Brooke, Nesto, and Paige join us?"

"Of course, Kade. I always make plenty."

Clive waited until she was down the stairs before pulling out his phone, looking at Kade. "I got a call from J.D. Montalban. You remember him?"

"Sure do. Been a while since we've connected. What's he up to?"

"About the time you left, the agency put him in deep with the Montalvo-Ortiz cartel. Pulled him out a week ago when things went south. I didn't tell him much, enough to pique his interest. He's got a bunch of time coming and offered to help."

J.D. was one of the best. Kade couldn't ask for a better team to figure it all out. "How soon can he be here?"

"Tomorrow."

"Call him. I'll be downstairs with Brooke. When you're finished, I'll take you out to Nesto's cabin so you can talk with him and Paige."

Clive's brow lifted. "I heard she broke things off."

Kade shook his head. "Yeah, she did. They aren't back together. Since it involves the family, Nesto's helping her out. Even though both of us were with Paige today, Javé still got to her. She doesn't like it, but she'll be staying with Nesto until this is all sorted out. I'll see if you and J.D. can stay in her cabin while you're here."

"Whatever works, man. You head downstairs to be with your lady and I'll call J.D."

Bounding down the steps, Kade headed to the kitchen where Brooke spoke with her mother. They'd always been close, but the death of her father years before tightened the bond. It had been a blessing when Annie met Heath. Brooke, Cam, and Eric, as well as Heath's children, Trey and Cassie, showed no hesitancy in accepting the union, bringing the two families together.

"Thanks for letting Clive stay here, Annie."

Waving her hand in the air, she shook her head. "No need for thanks. He's welcome any time. Brooke told me about what happened with Paige today. Is she all right?"

"A little shaken, but she's a strong woman. She's staying with Nesto until this all goes away." Kade opened the refrigerator door, pulling out a bottle of water.

"If I had my way, those kids would be living together permanently." Annie placed the roast in the oven, closing the door. "It would be a real shame if they aren't able to get past this and build a life together."

Brooke glanced at Kade. Both felt the same way, knowing it would take a lot of time and a minor miracle for Nesto to put the pain behind him. The fact he had another woman in the background didn't bode well for Paige.

"You know, Nesto's been seeing someone."

"Piffles." Annie waved her hand in the air again. "I'm sure she's a nice lady, but no one is going to replace Paige in his heart. Given enough time, he'll figure it out."

Kade laughed. "Piffles? Well, you must be pretty certain if you're bringing *that* out."

Annie stopped cutting vegetables, settling her hands on the counter. "Like you, Nesto's been through a lot. The same way Brooke healed your heart, Paige did the same for him. Her actions may have been misplaced, but she made the decisions for the right reasons. I think Nesto is smart enough not to let pride get in the way. Don't you?"

Kade had no answer. Slipping an arm around Brooke's waist, he kissed her cheek, hoping Annie was right.

Paige stared at the ceiling, her arms above her head, legs stretched out. She'd retreated into her bedroom an hour before, changed into sleeping pants and a tank top, her head spinning from another round of questions at dinner. Clive had been persistent, forcing her to recount small details she hadn't remembered when describing the incident with Javé to Nesto and Kade. She hoped those specifics mattered.

Pressing fingers against her temples, she closed her eyes, trying not to think of where Nesto had gone. Right now, Clive sat in the living room, watching television as he played babysitter during Nesto's absence. She'd heard him mention the name Val before he left, thinking she'd already tucked herself away in her room. Paige didn't want to accept he'd moved on, but reality had a way of killing fantasies.

Standing, she checked her image in the mirror, then grabbed one of Nesto's long-sleeved shirts from the guest room closet, slipping it on. Watching a meaningless show might distract her enough to rid her mind of Nesto. Opening the door, she took the few steps to the living room.

"Do you mind company?"

Standing, Clive gave her a weary smile. "Not at all. I'm watching some comedy." He named a couple actors she didn't recognize. "You can select whatever you want. I'm not picky." He held out the remote.

She sat down in the leather chair Nesto preferred—a lounger with electric controls. "Whatever you're watching is fine. I can't seem to sleep, even though I'm exhausted. Maybe a movie will help."

"A glass of wine might do the same." He held up his empty bottle of beer. "Nesto has an open bottle of red in the refrigerator."

"That'd be great." She watched as he poured her a glass, then grabbed another beer for himself, his movements graceful for such a tall man. He wasn't broad like Nesto, but wiry with corded muscles in his arms. She had no doubt Clive could take care of himself in any situation.

"You did real well remembering details. Most victims are too flustered to recall much." He handed her the glass, then lowered himself onto the sofa.

She shrugged, taking a sip of wine. "Funny, I never thought of myself as a victim."

"I don't think it's in your nature to act like one. You handled yourself well, didn't break down or run. Nesto is proud of you."

Her head snapped toward him at the comment. "Don't kid yourself, Clive. Nesto doesn't think much of me at all. I'm only staying in his cabin because of the threat. Once it's over, I'll be back in my cabin and he'll have his freedom back."

Clive set down his beer, leaning forward, resting his arms on his legs. "I may be misreading him, but I doubt Nesto sees you as a burden."

She sighed, staring at the images on the TV. "Don't get me wrong. I'm grateful he's willing to play bodyguard. Especially after what happened yesterday. I also know

Nesto has a personal life he's putting on hold because of me."

Clive nodded. "I see." Leaning back, he stretched his arms across the back of the sofa. She could almost see his mind working. Underneath his laidback persona, she guessed there hid a complicated man who'd seen a lot and spoke sparingly.

Standing, she grabbed the remote, increasing the volume, then sat down. "Let's see how good your taste in movies is, Agent Nelson."

An hour later, Paige wiped tears from her eyes, her stomach still convulsing in laughter. The movie had been perfect, her appreciation for it growing as she finished another glass of wine.

She hadn't thought of Nesto or who he was with since she'd turned up the volume. Sometime during the movie, she'd moved to sit at the other end of the sofa from Clive, her legs propped on the coffee table, then tucked under her as she relaxed.

"Great choice, Clive. I can't believe the guy..." She thought of a particular scene and started laughing all over again.

Clive joined her. "I know which one you mean."

The door opened, Nesto walking in, coming to an abrupt stop at the scene before him. Paige sat cross-legged next to Clive, her face flushed with laughter. The old chambray shirt she wore barely covered the thin tank top and lightweight pajama pants. She and Clive were carrying on so much, they didn't even notice him until he cleared his throat.

Clive stood, picking up the empty beer bottles and Paige's empty wine glass. "Hey, man. Did you have a good evening?"

He glared at Clive, then Paige. "Appears you two had a much better time than me."

Standing, she barely acknowledged Nesto as she walked toward her room. "I'm sure *Val* gave you a real good time," she mumbled, wishing she'd gotten into bed before he came home. She didn't need to see the satisfied look on his face placed there by another woman.

Resting his hands on his hips, he watched her walk away. "What the hell's wrong with her?"

Clive leaned against the counter, crossing his arms. "Don't know. I got the impression she knew you went to see Val. It didn't sit well with her."

Muttering a curse, Nesto moved past him, grabbed a bottle of water, and guzzled it. "It's not what she's thinking."

Clive held up his hands. "Not my problem." Heading to the door, he grabbed the knob, then turned. "Seems you two have a lot of unfinished business. Might be a good time to work it out."

Watching as Clive closed the door, Nesto grabbed the remote, sinking into the lounger, surfing the channels. After a few minutes, he realized he hadn't looked at a single show, his mind consumed with thoughts of Paige.

He'd spoken to Clive after dinner, realizing he had to get away after bringing Paige back to the cabin. Meaning to take a long drive, he ended up at Val's apartment. Walking up the path, he believed losing himself in the beautiful redhead would be the best way to push Paige from his mind.

Instead, when Val opened the door and let him in, he realized this wasn't where he wanted to be and she wasn't the woman he desired. He felt uncomfortable stringing her along, giving her the impression there could ever be more.

An hour later, he drove away, leaving a gracious, although hurt woman standing at her front door. He'd been right to make the break. Val had hoped for more, and Nesto knew she deserved a man who could give it to her.

After another hour of driving around, he pulled to a stop in front of the cabin, determined to talk with Paige, even if he had to wake her up.

Seeing her laughing, relaxed, enjoying her time with Clive hit him with the intensity of a punch to the solar plexus. Nesto wanted to be the man sitting next to her, laughing, pulling her close. He just hadn't been able to get past the belief she'd walk out again when things got hard or when her parents applied pressure to get their way. Nesto was a selfish man. He needed to know his woman was all in, the same as he would be when he made the commitment.

Tossing the television remote aside, he stalked to his room, glancing at her closed door, wondering if she'd answer if he knocked. Scrubbing a hand down his face, he shook his head. Tonight wasn't the right time.

The sound of her phone had Paige reaching toward the table, fumbling with it before putting it to her ear.

"It's Paul."

She shot up, resting her back against the headboard. "Where are you?"

"Staying at some janky motel in northern Phoenix. When I got to town, I got a call from my business partner that had me going underground." She waited as he drew in a deep breath, wondering if he held a cigarette or something stronger. "I've got to see you, Paige. Today. I'll drive up, meet you wherever you want."

"All right, but I won't be coming alone. Nesto will be with me."

"Not a chance, sis. He's a fed. I don't trust him."

The battle within her swelled. Paul was her brother, her own flesh and blood. Still, she'd made a promise to Nesto. She had to make a choice.

"Well, I *do* trust him. It's either Nesto and me or you're on your own." Her heart pounded as she waited, hearing his deep breathing on the other end of the line.

"Fine. I'll call you when I get to Fire Mountain." He hung up before she could respond.

Setting the phone on the table, she threw off the blankets, slipping into the shirt she'd worn the night before. Opening her door, she heard nothing from Nesto's bedroom as she stepped into the bathroom, turning on the water.

Letting her clothes fall to the floor, she relaxed as the hot water washed down her back. Putting a small amount of shampoo on her hair, she scrubbed it into her scalp, rinsing before using the body wash. Turning up the heat, she closed her eyes, resting her hands against the back wall to let the hot water soothe her taut muscles.

The sound of running water should've stopped him. She'd thought he'd been with another woman, probably wouldn't welcome what he offered. Nesto pushed the thought aside, hesitating an instant before pushing the door open, slipping out of his briefs before stepping in behind her. Paige gasped at the feel of his hands on her bare skin, her body tensing.

"What are you doing in here?" Her voice shook, feeling his breath against the side of her neck.

Nipping the sensitive skin below her ear, he pulled her closer to his chest, not answering.

"You shouldn't be here." She moaned as his hands moved across her body, warm water sluicing over both of them.

"Tell me to leave and I will." He sucked on the delicate skin at the junction of her shoulder and neck, hearing another low moan escape. "Say it, Paige. Tell me to go and I'll be out of here." Turning her to face him, he captured her mouth, doing things he'd only dreamed of for months. "Say it."

"I can't. I don't want you to go," she breathed out, feeling his hands work their magic on all her sensitive places.

He chuckled into her mouth. "I didn't think so." Touching her in ways he knew she liked, he pleasured her, feeling his own body respond.

"Nesto, please..."

"Please what? Tell me what you want, sweetheart." His hands and mouth continued their merciless onslaught, Paige squirming in his arms, restless and needy. "Say it. What do you want me to do?" He could feel the instant she relaxed in his arms, giving up the battle of wills she'd been fighting with herself.

"I'm so tired of being without you. I need you, Nesto. Please..." She tightened her arms around his neck, twisting her fingers in his hair, taking everything he gave and returning the same.

Pulling back, he waited until she opened her eyes, his heart pounding at what he saw. The same love as before she'd left him showed on her face, providing renewed life to a man who'd been drowning without her. Unable to accept what he saw, Nesto turned her around.

"Place your hands on the wall." His words were harsh against her ear. A growl escaped him, pleased when she didn't resist. "That's it, baby. Just like that." Aligning himself behind her, he gave her what she wanted, what he needed, then collapsed behind her.

Paige sat on the edge of her bed, the towel still wrapped around her, face buried in her hands. Sobs echoed in the small bedroom, forcing her to confront all she'd lost. She cried for what they'd had, for breaking his heart, for the anguish in his eyes when he'd left the shower, dressed, then walked out without another word.

She'd confessed how much she still loved him, her regret over not talking to him before making the decision to walk away. Her words seemed to have little effect. He didn't look at her again before slipping into his clothes, shutting the door behind him.

Chapter Eleven

Outside the cabin, Nesto sat on a well-used Adirondack chair, watching the sun finish its rise over the eastern mountains, a deep ache in his heart. No doubt about it, he'd been an ass to take Paige the way he had and then walk out.

Cursing himself as every kind of fool, he sucked in a deep breath of fresh morning air, knowing he had to apologize. Nesto had taken his doubt, confusion, and anger out on Paige. When she'd broken down, telling him she still loved him, he'd lost it. The deep sobs when he left sliced through his heart. He wondered how a man and woman could love so much while causing each other such acute pain.

Standing, he opened the door, seeing Paige's back to him as she made coffee. Tensing at his approach, she stilled when he placed his hands on her shoulders. Leaning down, Nesto kissed the spot below her ear, feeling her tremble in response.

"I'm sorry, Paige. I didn't mean to hurt you."

She shifted around so quickly, he didn't have a chance to respond before she shoved his chest, pushing him away.

"That's a lie, Nesto. You *did* mean to hurt me, punish me for what I did to you...to us." She swiped at tears pooling in her eyes, her expression tight. Trying to slip past him, she stopped when he gripped her arm.

"We need to talk."

"Why? So you can tell me it was a mistake, that you're heading back to see Val tonight? Forget it. I can't even look at you right now."

He didn't let go, gently pulling her back to him, wrapping his arms around her. Tucking her into his chest, he rested his chin on her head.

"When I left last night, I drove over to Val's. I had every intention of losing myself in her." Feeling Paige try to pull away, he tightened his hold. "Instead, I broke things off."

Nesto waited, hoping she'd say something, anything, to help him find clarity in the mass of confusion. When she didn't, he continued.

"I don't know how to go back, Paige. All my life, I've moved forward, certain of my path, filled with confidence. Everything changed when you left. Now you're back and I don't know how to respond, what to say. I keep asking myself if we can have a second chance, then wonder if I even want one. You've got me going in circles."

Leaning back, she looked up at him. "Why?"

Letting out a deep sigh, he rested his forehead against hers. "There's one woman I want, and it isn't Val. The problem is I don't know if I can find a way to trust you again." Dipping his head, he kissed the tip of her nose. "I want to, Paige, I just…"

Her heart squeezed at the strain in Nesto's voice, the doubt that haunted him. She'd hurt him worse than she'd ever imagined. Drawing in a shaky breath, she tightened her arms around him.

"It wasn't a lie, telling you how much I still love you. There's no reason to believe me, but the horrible mistake I made with Paul, choosing to help him over staying with you, will never happen again. It's a huge leap of faith. If I were in your place, I don't know if I could do it. All I'm asking is for you to consider giving us another chance."

Nesto wanted to trust her more than he needed his next breath. He just wasn't ready to cross the line. Nuzzling her neck, he trailed kisses along her jaw, brushed his mouth across hers.

"I've missed you so damn much, Paige," he breathed out. "I'm just not ready to make any promises."

The comment hurt, but it also reminded her of one of the many reasons she loved him. Promises were precious, and Nesto didn't offer them without knowing they'd be kept.

"Then we can take it a day at a time. As slow as you need until you're certain of your feelings. If you find you can't get over the past, tell me and I'll walk away."

His stomach clenched at the thought of losing her again. At least her offer gave them time to find out if they could still build a future.

He looked down at her. "A day at a time works for me. When do you want to start?"

Leaning up, she kissed him again, letting her lips brush down his jaw and neck, feeling his body stiffen. "Can we start now?"

Tilting his head in question, he smiled when her meaning became clear. "Are you sure?"

"It's been too long since you've made love to me, Nesto. The shower, well...that was just sex. Not the image I want to remember."

Glancing at the clock, he scooped her into his arms. "Then we'll wipe it right out of your mind."

"I think I heard Kade and Brooke already head to the office." Paige glanced at Nesto as he drove to work, her face flushed from their lovemaking. She hadn't felt so good in a long time.

"He texted me." He smirked. "You were taking another shower."

Reaching over, she slapped his arm. "Funny. What did you text back?"

"The usual. I told him I had my woman in bed and he'd have to deal with it."

Sitting up straight, her eyes widened, the flush turning to a red glow. "You didn't."

Chuckling, he leaned over, grasping her hand. "You're right. Said we were running late and to go ahead."

Sitting back, she closed her eyes before they popped open when she remembered the call from her brother. "Paul called. He'll be in Fire Mountain tonight and wants to meet."

Nesto pulled to the side of the road and stopped, turning to look at her. "And you're just telling me now?"

She blew out a breath, glaring at him as a blush crept up her cheeks. "He called early, right before I got in the shower. Things got a little crazy after that."

Resting his left arm on the steering wheel, he grinned. "Yeah, they did."

She would've slugged him if he wasn't so damn handsome and didn't make her heart trip over itself. "Don't you want to know what I told him?"

"What?" His chest tightened, hoping she hadn't agreed to meet him alone.

"I told him you'd be coming with me." Her gaze narrowed. "That's what we agreed to, right?"

Relaxing, Nesto nodded. "It's exactly what I wanted. Kade and Clive will also come along."

"I don't think so. It might scare him off."

"They'll drive in a separate car, but they will be joining us. I'm sorry, but I don't trust him not to set up an ambush. We know Paul is dancing to the Sons' tune right now, and I wouldn't put it past him to do something foolish, such as promise to turn you over so Javé can persuade you to intervene with the MacLarens."

Paige shook her head, not wanting to believe Paul would put her in such danger. "He would never..." She paused, accepting her brother might very well hand her over to Javé and his gang. "I just don't understand what happened to the sweet boy I grew up with."

Shifting forward, Nesto edged back onto the road. "Drugs are nothing but evil, Paige. Your brother decided to accept them with clear eyes and greedy hands. It's good you have those memories. I'm afraid what's happening now isn't going to be something you'll want to remember."

Thursday flew by without a call from Paul. Kade, Nesto, and Clive sequestered themselves in a small conference room, talking to contacts, devising a plan to keep everyone safe. J.D. Montalban arrived after lunch, joining them to share his own information.

"What do you think they're discussing now?" Brooke looked through the glass wall into the room where the four men talked. "They've been in there for hours."

Paige stared at Nesto as they walked past, admiring the way his dress shirt stretched across his taut muscles. Her heart expanded, remembering how he looked without the shirt. They hadn't had more than an hour in his bed that morning, but he'd made the most of it, leaving them both exhausted and sated.

"Nesto mentioned J.D.'s last assignment gave him some insight into the Montalvo-Ortiz cartel. Last night, Clive told me he has data he can share about the Devil's Sons motorcycle club." Paige turned into the employee lounge and pulled a diet soda from the refrigerator. "Nesto also said Kade heard back from Thad Montgomery. Do you know him?"

Brooke shook her head. "Not really. He was with the DEA the same time as Kade. Thad provided a lot of help with the problem in Houston a few months ago."

"Anyway, I guess Thad found out some things and wanted a conference call with the guys today."

Brooke followed her back down the hall, slowing her pace as they passed the small conference room again. Not one of the guys looked up, too engrossed in their own discussion to notice anyone else.

Paige popped the top of the soda can, taking a long swallow. "I'm sure it must be hard for Clive and J.D., wanting to share what they know without jeopardizing their jobs."

Brooke drank from her water bottle, nodding at Paige's hand. "You do know that stuff is bad for you, right?"

She looked at the can, then shook her head, smirking. "I've got a motorcycle club, my own brother, and maybe the cartel threatening me. Do you think I care about drinking soda?"

Laughing, Brooke pushed open the door to the conference room to rejoin the main group. "No, probably not."

"I think it's the only way to approach this, Nesto. Find out what they want, then figure a way to use it against them." J.D. tapped his pen on the table, his mind working through various scenarios.

"It depends on what Javé wants from Paige." Nesto's head throbbed at the amount of information Clive and J.D. had provided, compliments of their boss, the same man Kade reported to before leaving the agency.

Clive wanted the ability to talk freely with Kade and Nesto. It had been touchy at first, trying to talk the by-the-book suit into going along with the plan. He'd relented after insisting on some stiff stipulations and making a comment about being on their own if things went south.

Kade leaned back in his chair, rubbing his chin. "If he's asking for an introduction to one of the executives, it will be up to the brothers to make the decision. My guess is either Pops or Heath will fight it out to be the ones to meet with them."

"Not Jace?" Nesto asked.

"Heath and my dad have a real personal stake in this. Their children have been threatened, which is something they won't abide. Jace's boys, Blake and Brett, are away at college, safe from the reach of the Sons."

"For now." Clive stood, walking to the window to gaze out on the expansive view. "Javé wants to target one MacLaren business, using it to distribute whatever product they're moving. In return, he and the cartel will agree to do no harm to the family. If not, they'll start targeting individuals until the MacLarens agree to help them."

Cursing, Nesto tossed his pen onto the table, shredding a hand through his hair. "Why the MacLarens? Of all the companies, why would they choose them?"

"The Santiago family, Nesto." Kade joined Clive at the window. "There's a feud within the cartel between the original family and the Santiagos. Ivan's concerned it's going to erupt sooner rather than later with a lot of blood spilled."

J.D. looked at him. "Explain."

"It goes way back. The Santiago family and the Montalvo-Ortiz cartel started out working together. Not in drugs. Most likely guns and human trafficking. A feud started and the Santiagos lost the fight. Ivan's uncles, Stefan and Octavio, somehow worked their way back in, promising who knows what to the cartel. It all went well until they tried using Double Ace to move guns. When that blew apart, Stefan and Octavio went into hiding, practically giving their ownership in Double Ace to Ivan. It wasn't enough for the cartel, though. They're out to punish them for their failure. As you know, there's a strong bond between some of the Santiagos, who disassociated themselves from the cartel years ago, and the MacLarens."

"Your mother is a Santiago, right, Kade?" J.D. asked.

"She is. Ivan Santiago is my cousin and Gage Templeton's business partner. Gage and Skye MacLaren plan to marry in a few weeks." Kade scrubbed a hand down his face. "It's a freaking mess, one the cartel and Javé plan to exploit."

Clive clasped him on the shoulder. "It's not going to happen, man. I've got a sixth sense about this stuff, and I think Paige coming to Fire Mountain has provided the link we've been waiting for to bring the Sons down and put a dent in the cartel's activity."

"It's *never* enough to close them, though. Is it, Clive?" Nesto asked.

"Nope, but I've learned any win is one I'll take."

"One more item we haven't discussed."

"What's that, Kade?" J.D. asked.

"I know you have information on Satan's Brethren. I want to know what you've got."

J.D. snorted. "Sorry, amigo. That club is off the table."

Kade glanced at Nesto, their eyes locking. After a moment, he switched his gaze back to J.D. "You've got something big on them, don't you?"

Holding up his hands, he shook his head. "Don't go there. Let's work on what we have."

"Right now, that's nothing. Not until Javé or Paul contact Paige again." Nesto's gut twisted when he thought of the danger to her. "How could a woman as good as her be caught in this mess?"

Kade looked at him. "Love for family, bro. It's a blessing and a curse."

Nesto walked Paige to the truck, keeping his hands to himself until they were settled inside. She gasped when he reached over, snaking an arm around her waist to drag her across the seat.

"I've waited all day for this." His mouth descended on hers, capturing it with a greedy need borne from months of being without her.

Wrapping her arms around his neck, Paige gave it back to him, squirming to get closer in the confines of the truck. A pounding on the window had them pulling apart. Sucking in a breath, Nesto scowled at Kade, who stood there with a smirk on his face.

He opened the door. "What do you want?"

"You do know everyone coming out of the building can see you two, right?"

Nesto blew out a breath, his shoulders slumping. "Well, damn."

"I know the feeling. J.D. and Clive are going with Brooke and me to dinner. Join us."

"That would be great," Paige said, earning a frown from Nesto.

Overruled, he nodded. "We'll follow you."

Chapter Twelve

"Hey, sleepyhead. We need to shower and get to work." Nesto used a finger to push hair off Paige's face, then kissed her forehead.

Groaning, she opened one eye. "Is it morning already?"

Chuckling, he threw off the covers, swatting her lightly on her backside. "It's almost eight."

Sitting up, she gasped when she saw the time. "We overslept." Jumping out of bed, she grabbed the first thing she saw, Nesto's t-shirt from the day before, and ran into the bath. "I'll be quick." Sending him a warning look, she started to close the door. "And don't even think about joining me."

Nesto didn't move from the bed, a smile curving his mouth. This was how their mornings used to be back in San Diego, before the call from her parents changed their lives. The thought had his smile slipping. As much as he wanted to fall into the same routine, he couldn't allow himself the luxury. Lowering his defenses, letting her control his heart, had to wait. He needed time, and so did Paige, even if she didn't believe it.

"Okay. Your turn." Rubbing her hair with a towel, she walked into the bedroom, his t-shirt covering her to above her knees. She didn't notice the wary look on his face or how the playful way he'd woken her had vanished. "Hey." She stopped next to him. "It's your turn."

Blinking, he nodded. "Yeah. I'll be out in a minute. We can get coffee at the office."

Paige watched him disappear into the bathroom, wondering what had dampened his mood. She suspected worry over Javé, Paul, the cartel—possibly all three. He had a lot of responsibility on any given day. Her presence had done nothing to lighten the load.

Drying her hair, she rubbed moisturizer on her face, added blush, then slipped into gray pants and a light coral top. Fastening on a necklace and earrings, she turned when Nesto walked in, a towel around his waist. Her eyes darkened as he made his way toward her.

"I've seen that look before." Leaning down, he kissed her, lingering longer than he should. "You'll just have to wait until tonight to get what you want."

Her brow lifted as she reached out, loosening the towel so it slid to the floor. "I love unwrapping presents."

Shaking his head, Nesto stepped away. "You're going to have to wait until later to play with this present, babe."

He dressed quickly, grabbing her hand as they walked outside. Clive's car was gone from Paige's cabin, where he and J.D. were staying. The night before, she'd moved most of her clothes into the guest closet of his cabin. He didn't know how he felt about the fact she didn't even ask to move them into his closet.

Ten minutes later, they entered the building, breaking apart as she walked to her office and he joined Kade, J.D., and Clive for another day of analyzing and working through various scenarios. They needed to hear from Paul or Javé soon, before the agents had to return to their regular jobs.

Stopping for a cup of coffee, Nesto stepped back into the hallway, halting when Paige called his name, holding up her phone as she hurried toward him.

"It's Paul. He wants to meet for lunch." She tapped the speaker icon.

Nodding, he mouthed *where* and *when.*

"All right. Where would you like us to meet you?"

"A place called the Tavern. Do you know it?"

"It's a sports bar not too far from my office. What time?"

"Noon. You and your boyfriend. No one else."

She scowled at the phone. "His name is Ernesto, Paul."

"Fine, whatever. I'll see you at noon."

She hung up, letting out a pent-up breath, her shoulders relaxing. "What if he brings Javé?"

"Kade, Clive, and J.D. will be watching." He placed an arm around her shoulders. "Trust me, babe. We'll be safe, even if Javé does show up. In fact, it might be good to get both of them there at one time so we can sort this out sooner. I don't like having Paul as a go-between."

"I know you don't want to hear this, but I'm still hoping there's a way to get Paul out of this life."

"First, we have to keep him alive, which won't be easy given his connection with the Sons. Second, Paul has to want to get out of the drug trade. So far, I've seen no evidence of him wanting to change. I'm afraid he may be one of the people hooked on the lifestyle as much as the drugs themselves."

She looked up at him, a desperate expression in her eyes. "Paul swears he isn't using."

Tilting his head, Nesto raised his brows. "It's up to you if you want to believe him. Me? I'm a skeptic by nature. There's a lot your brother has to make up for to get clean in my mind." He dropped his arm as some other employees walked past them. "I'd better get with the others and set this up. I'll come by your office a little before noon."

Paige nodded, her face tense.

Lifting her chin, he studied her face. "Are you all right? I can meet with Paul alone if you aren't up for it."

Stepping away, she shook her head. "Of course I'm up for it. I just hope he isn't setting us up."

A sad grin crossed his face. "Oh, he's setting us up, sweetheart. He just doesn't know the hammer is going to come down on him first."

Paige's hands shook as they walked into the sports bar not far from the office. The Tavern had been a local favorite for years, serving craft and commercial beer, hamburgers, sandwiches, and salads, as patrons enjoyed events on several large screens. She'd been inside before, but under different circumstances. Nesto rested his hand on the small of her back, looking around the darkened interior. Not seeing Paul, he guided her to a table in back.

"Are you all right?" Nesto pulled out Paige's chair.

Nodding, she sat down, her gaze darting around the half-full space as Nesto took a seat next to her. "He isn't here."

"Be patient. He'll show up."

"What do we do if Javé is with him?"

Nesto grasped her hand and squeezed, his voice softening. "No change in plans, sweetheart. We listen to what they have to say, making no promises. We want to keep them talking, learn as much as possible about who's involved." Spotting Paul walk through the door, he let go of Paige's hand. "Don't worry. I'm here with you, and the others are outside."

Paul didn't speak as he sat across from them. He placed his hands on the table, clasping them tightly. Nesto noticed the shaking, the fear in his eyes. As agreed, neither he nor Paige spoke, waiting for Paul to start the conversation.

He glanced up, ignoring Nesto to focus on Paige. "Thanks for coming."

Paige started to respond, then stopped when the waitress walked up, took their orders, then left. "What's going on, Paul?"

He switched his gaze to Nesto, studying him as one would size up an enemy. "I thought you two were over."

Paige leaned forward. "The situation between Nesto and me isn't why we're here. I need to know what's happening with you."

Paul drew in a shaky breath, nodding at the waitress as she set down their drinks and walked away. Bringing the bottle of beer to his lips, he took a long swallow.

"My business partners are pressuring me to expand distribution of their products. They've learned of your connection to the MacLarens and want you to set up a meeting with them."

Paige shifted in her chair, keeping to the plan she and Nesto had discussed. "I already know one of your partners is Javé Cruz. He called my private phone and introduced himself."

Paul glanced away, his mouth drawing into a thin line. "I should've warned you."

"Well, you didn't. I gather Javé isn't your only partner. Who are the others?"

"They aren't important. It's Javé we have to satisfy and he wants a private meeting with one of the brothers. Heath, Jace, or Rafe. Any of the three will do."

Paige sat back in her chair. "How do you know their names?"

He smirked. "It wasn't hard. A quick internet search led me to pages of information on them. Heath is the chairman. Rafe and Jace share the CEO position. They've got their hands in a wide range of businesses. Javé wants to speak with them about one."

"Here you are. Sorry it took a little longer than normal." The waitress smiled. "A new cook training in the kitchen."

None of the three dug into the food, silence stretching between them until Nesto picked up his burger and took a bite. Chewing, he washed it down with the soda he'd ordered.

"The MacLarens will want to know all the players, Paul. Don't underestimate them. They'll know Javé and his club aren't the only ones involved." Nesto popped a french fry into his mouth, taking his time, letting Paul consider what he'd said. "I'll warn you. They won't do anything illegal, and they don't take kindly to threats. I can't imagine what Javé could offer to persuade them to help an outlaw gang."

Paul's burger stopped halfway to his mouth. Setting it down, his expression showed the first signs of regret. "I don't know what Javé has in mind. All I know is he wants to have a meeting." Pushing the plate away, he stood, looking at Paige. "I'll call you Monday. That should give you enough time to approach the MacLarens, encourage one of them to see the advantage of meeting with Javé."

Paige watched him walk out, her shoulders slumping. "We didn't learn anything, did we?"

"We confirmed what we already expected. Paul's working for Javé, the Sons want to use one of the MacLaren businesses for illegal purposes, and there are definitely other partners. Now comes the hard part."

"What's that?"

"Telling the MacLarens."

"No better time than the present." Kade glanced at Paige, who sat at the table in the small conference room. Nesto sat next to her, Clive and J.D. across the table. "It's Friday afternoon and all three are still in their offices."

Paige looked at Nesto. "I'd like to get this over with."

He nodded, pulling out his phone. "Heath, it's Nesto."

A few minutes later, everyone convened in Heath's office, listening to Nesto and Paige. Kade, Clive, and J.D. nodded, confirming what they'd heard through the wire Paige wore when meeting her brother.

Rafe ran a hand through his dark hair, shaking his head. "I don't understand why they're coming after us. A legitimate business with no ties to anything illegal."

J.D. answered. "It isn't all that unusual, Mr. MacLaren. Criminal gangs look for every possible way to move their product. They aren't above using coercion to get what they want. It *is* unusual for them to target a company as large and as high profile as MacLaren Enterprises."

"We have something they want," Kade said.

Rafe narrowed his gaze at his son. "What's that?"

"Our existing operation for moving stock between the States, Canada, and Mexico, Pops. I think they've learned of our interest in acquiring Double Ace. Even after the issues of a few months ago, they probably still see it as a prime way to move their product across borders."

The room quieted as the brothers considered what to do next.

"Options?" Heath asked.

"Ignore the request and continue business as usual. We'll continue with additional security and bodyguards until we believe Javé has given up and moved on. Or accept the invitation to meet and find out what he wants." Nesto rested his arms on the table. "You might be able to discover more about the other partners."

"Or he may make a direct threat, which Clive and J.D. could use in their ongoing case against the Sons and cartel." Kade looked at his two former colleagues, who returned slight nods.

"Then I'll meet with them."

Rafe smacked a hand on the table. "To hell with that, Heath. I'll go. It's my connection to the Santiago family that has put us in their crosshairs."

"Not a chance, Rafe. Don't make me pull rank on you."

A smirked crossed Rafe's face. "We could fight for it, Heath. The same as we did when we were kids."

"No need for that." Everyone looked at Jace. "I'm going to the meeting and that's the end of it." When Heath tried to speak, Jace held up his hand. "Hear me out. Nesto and Kade have already said they don't believe there's danger in going to the meeting. But they could be wrong. If anything happens, the two of you need to keep things going." He looked between his brothers, seeing the indecision on their faces. "Let me do this. Unless you don't think I'm capable of handling it."

"Sonofabitch," Heath grumbled. "Of course you're capable enough. As the oldest brother, and chairman, it's my job to handle threats to the company."

Jace shook his head. "Not this time, big brother." He looked at Nesto, then Paige. "You tell Paul I'm willing to meet Javé, listen to his business proposal with no guarantees we'll do anything he asks. You figure out where and when."

Kade cleared his throat. "Nesto will be in the meeting with you, Jace. Clive, J.D., and I will be nearby. We'll talk more about what to expect once we have a time and place."

Heath stood, shoving his hands into his pockets. "I don't like it, Jace. It should be me."

"Don't begrudge me a little excitement, Heath. With Blake and Brett away at college, I'm the right person for this. Besides, look at the backup I have." He swept his hand toward Kade, Nesto, Clive, and J.D. "Think of it as a simple meet and greet, just like the monthly Chamber of Commerce meetings."

Rafe snorted. "Like it will be that simple."

Paige kept her afternoon schedule of acquisition meetings. The purchase of Double Ace had been seen as a given when the review began. Even though the team hadn't been told to hold off on a recommendation, she couldn't help but think it would be wise to wait.

"Paige?"

She glanced up at Brooke. "I'm sorry. What did you say?"

"I thought you could work with Sean on Serenity, and I'd work with Matt on Champion Horse Breeding. It will help to speed the process along. With all that's happened, we need to gain some ground in order to give the brothers a recommendation by the end of next week."

"Sure, Brooke. Should I go find Sean now?"

Brooke looked at her, noting the lines of worry. "You know, it's already past five. Why don't you go find Nesto, have dinner, and unwind a bit? Unless things have changed, the family is planning a trail ride tomorrow, sometime after Kade, Nesto, and Matt work the new horses. Afterward, there's to be a barbeque at the ranch house. Annie, Caroline, and Reyna have been preparing food all day. It'll do us all good to kick back and relax."

"Nesto hadn't mentioned anything about tomorrow. Sounds good, though. I can't remember the last time I went riding."

"Wish I could go along. Unfortunately, the doctor has taken it off my list of approved activities."

"How's it going in here?" Nesto walked in, resting his hand on the back of Paige's chair.

Brooke closed her laptop. "We're just finishing up for the night. Why don't you take Paige to dinner, get her away from this place?"

He settled a hand on Paige's shoulder. "I'm not going to argue. If you're ready, Paige, we can leave anytime."

Standing, she gathered her laptop and notes. "I'll see you tomorrow, Brooke."

Walking to the truck, Nesto held her hand, glancing around the parking lot, feeling a small measure of relief when he had her safe in the passenger seat. He didn't believe Javé would try anything at this point. The Sons president wanted a meeting with the MacLarens, not push them away by hurting one of their employees.

Closing his door, he started the engine, then looked at her. "You did real good today. I know you've been through a lot the last few days."

She reached over, resting a hand on his thigh. "I'm glad you were there. It made it a lot easier."

He wanted to tell her he'd always be there for her, she'd never again have to carry her burdens alone. Instead, he placed his hand over hers and squeezed.

"It's been a long week. Let's get some dinner."

Chapter Thirteen

At eight the next morning, Nesto stood in the middle of the round pen, using the lunge line to exercise one of the new horses. He'd done this often in high school, working as a part-time wrangler, and enjoyed doing it when he wasn't traveling between companies. This morning, he planned to exercise one horse before the group left on the trail ride.

"You look pretty comfortable out there." Paige rested her arms on the top rung of the fence, watching Nesto guide the horse in circles, getting it to respond to his commands.

"It's amazing what I remembered after not doing this for over fifteen years. Like riding a bike, it comes back to you." With a slight verbal command and nudge of the lunge whip, the horse moved into a jog.

Nesto didn't mention the therapeutic nature of being in the ring in the early morning, just him and the animal. He'd spent many mornings out here, lunging horses, doing his best to forget Paige and move on. Today, she stood on the fence, a smile on her face. He still couldn't quite bring himself to believe it.

"I thought I heard you two drive up." Brooke joined her on the fence. "When I first met Kade and Nesto, I never pictured them as cowboys. After I saw them both ride, I wondered how they'd left it behind to join the army. They're naturals." She glanced to another round pen where Kade rode a horse he'd been working with for a few months.

The sound of engines caught their attention. Two trucks parked in the large gravel area near the house. Mitch, Dana, Sean, Gage, and Skye got out of one truck, Matt, Trey, and Cam got out of the other, striding toward them. Clive and J.D. had begged off, deciding to kick back at the cabin.

"How's the old man doing?" Sean leaned on the fence next to Paige, watching Nesto.

"I'm no expert, but the horse seems to be following the cues."

"Looks good to me." Sean lowered his cowboy hat, shielding his eyes from the sun. "Kade and Nesto used to break horses for the rancher they worked for in high school." He switched his gaze to the other pen, watching Kade for a few minutes. "Doesn't seem either one has forgotten much."

Paige looked over at him. "I forgot you don't have the chance to be around them much. You're kind of stuck off on your own."

"Yeah. I live at the dude ranch near Missoula, about two hundred miles from Crooked Tree. If the deal with Serenity goes through, I could be traveling between resorts in Montana, Wyoming, and Idaho. My guess is we'll close the camp for foster kids in Arizona and move it to one of the other locations." Sean watched Nesto lead the horse toward them.

"You here to help out or hit on Paige, Sean?" Nesto smiled at her, although she saw it didn't reach his eyes.

"Both, Nesto—if I can get away with it," Sean laughed. "What do you need me to do?"

"Help bring in and groom the horses we're riding today. I'll be there in a few minutes."

Sean touched two fingers to the brim of his hat and nodded before heading to the barn. Paige watched him go, grinning.

"He's a nice guy."

Nesto's comment had her shifting back toward him. "Yes, he is."

"I'm guessing most women find him attractive."

She nodded, hearing something in his voice she couldn't identify. "I suppose so."

He turned, leading the horse back to the barn. Paige jumped down from the fence, watching as he walked away, wondering what had gotten into him.

"Hey, Paige. Come with us. We're going to get our horses saddled." Mitch motioned for her to follow him, Dana, and the others.

Catching up to them, she looked around, then at Dana. "Where's Brooke?"

"Headed back into the house to help Annie prepare for the barbeque. She told us you haven't ridden in a long time."

"She's right."

Mitch grabbed Dana's hand as they entered the barn. "You're going with a bunch of people who grew up on horses, so there's nothing to worry about."

"Thanks, Dana. Nesto offered to ride alongside me on the trail."

Mitch stopped to look at her. "Are you two getting along all right? He can be a little overbearing."

Dana glanced at Paige. "That would be the pot calling the kettle black."

"Hey, I'm not overbearing. A little stubborn sometimes..." Mitch grinned at Dana as his voice trailed off.

"What has my older brother smiling?" Sean strolled up to them, slinging an arm around Paige's shoulders, winking at her.

"Dana and Mitch were discussing whether Mitch was stubborn or overbearing. He thinks—"

Her words were cut off by Sean's bark of laughter.

"Are you four ready to saddle your horses?" Nesto took a quick look at Paige and Sean before gesturing behind him. "Take your pick, but Paige will ride Rascal."

Sean dropped his arm from around her shoulders. "I'll help you saddle him, Paige. Come on."

Nesto narrowed his gaze at him. "I've got it covered, Sean." He nodded for her to follow him to a chestnut gelding. "Rascal is Annie's horse. He's a sweet mount." Running his hand along the horse's neck, he glanced up at Paige. "Ready to saddle him?"

She touched his arm, stopping him from grabbing the blanket. "What's going on, Nesto?"

Swiping his hat off his head, he glanced around, wishing he had a good answer. All he knew was when he saw her with Sean, something snapped inside him. His head told him Sean was being his usual self—friendly, flirty. What's more, he knew Paige just played along, nothing more. Settling his hat back in place, he shook his head.

"Nothing." Leaning down, he kissed her cheek, then moved past her to grab the blanket and saddle. Placing them on Rascal's back, he lifted the left stirrup, hooking it on the saddle horn. "This is how you cinch the saddle." He explained each step, making sure Paige understood. Finishing, he lowered the stirrup. "I'll adjust them once you're in the saddle." Bending, he cupped his hands together.

"Now?"

Standing, he grinned at her. "Yes, now." Again he cupped his hands. "Place your left foot in my hands, grab a fistful of mane with your left hand for balance, then swing your right leg over." When she hesitated, he glanced up. "Now would be good, Paige."

"Right." Sucking in a breath, Paige did as Nesto instructed, feeling a sense of accomplishment when she settled into the saddle.

Laying a hand on her thigh, his face broke into a warm grin. "How long since you've been on a horse?"

"Longer than I thought, but I'm fine now. In fact, I'm great."

Leading Rascal out to the others, he handed her the reins. "Hold them in your left hand. He's good at commands. When we're ready to go, squeeze him lightly with your lower legs, and keep your heels down. Mitch? Stay with her while I saddle Ghost. It won't take long."

"No problem." Mitch and Dana rode up next to her. "You good?"

Her left hand tightened on the reins, but she nodded. "Great."

"It'll be good to get away from what's going on. You do know we aren't going to let anything happen to you or any member of the family, right?"

She relaxed at his words, the sincerity in his voice. "Thanks, Mitch. You're right. It's been a long week, and it doesn't appear it's going to get any easier for a while. The truth is I'm more worried about the rest of you."

Mitch studied her, seeing the lines of worry around her eyes and mouth. "I'm sure Nesto has already told you we can take care of ourselves. Trust me...he's right."

Nesto reined up beside them. "I think we're all here. You ready, Paige?"

"Absolutely."

"Then let's go."

Kade and Sean rode in front through bush-lined trails, skirting large boulder formations into the national forest that shared a border with MacLaren land. Nesto didn't leave Paige's side, other than on trails too narrow for two horses. He marveled at the way she sat a horse. After the first thirty minutes, she relaxed, letting Rascal's movements guide the way her body responded in the saddle, transferring her weight for a smooth ride.

Every so often, Paige glanced at him, the radiance of her smile piercing a spot deep in his heart. It had been only a few days since they'd made an agreement to take their relationship day-to-day, giving him time to come to terms with what Paige had done.

Trust meant a great deal to Nesto. He didn't offer it blindly, and some people never earned it. All the men on his Special Forces team merited his respect and trust. He'd never considered giving it to a woman—until Paige. The fact she hadn't seen fit to confide in him about Paul, choosing to abandon their relationship rather than trust him, still ate at his heart.

They made love every night, held each other close until dawn, regaining the contentment he'd lost when she left. As much as he loved her, wanted to put the past behind them, he hadn't been able to take that step. With time, he hoped he could.

At noon, Kade and Mitch took a trail leading the group to a favorite Mexican restaurant. "We'll stop here for lunch."

Paige didn't wait for Nesto to assist her before sliding to the ground, rubbing her backside.

"I forgot to mention you'll probably be sore for a couple days. The more we ride, the easier it gets until you don't even notice it."

"I'd like that."

"What?" Nesto asked.

"Riding more. With you."

"Then we'll go as often as we can." Taking her hand, they followed the others inside. Juan Carlos greeted each of them, speaking in Spanish to Kade, then Nesto, before being introduced to Paige.

"It is a pleasure to meet you, señorita. Please, have a seat. I will bring you our homemade salsa and chips."

"This is very good." Paige took another bite of the enchilada-style burrito Juan Carlos suggested, following it with a few swallows of soda. "This place could become a habit."

"Kade and I come here whenever we're both in town." Nesto finished his chile rellenos, pushing the plate aside. Taking out his wallet, he pulled out some bills, passing them down the table to Mitch. "Looks like we're ready to start back."

Again, he took her hand as they returned to the horses. Nesto stood next to Rascal, ready to help Paige, when the distinct sound of motorcycles drew their attention. He studied the group, recognizing the Devil's Sons patches as they pulled into the lot. Mumbling a curse, he pushed Paige behind him, then locked eyes with Kade.

"Stay here."

"Wait, Nesto. I'll come with you."

"No, Paige. Let Kade and I speak with Javé." His stern look stilled Paige's movements. Without another word, he joined Kade, both moving to stand next to Javé's bike.

The president of Devil's Sons killed the engine, swung his leg over the bike, and crossed his arms. The club vice president and the sergeant-at-arms flanked him, smirks on each face.

"A MacLaren family gathering. I hope we didn't interrupt anything." Javé moved his gaze around the group, noting the men step in front of the women, their expressions grim. "A tight family. I can respect that."

Letting his arms drop to his sides, Javé walked up to Sean, a cocky grin spreading across his face as he regarded him. "Sean MacLaren. I'm told you work in Montana running a resort."

Sean's eyes narrowed, but he stayed quiet as Javé moved to Mitch.

"Mitch MacLaren. Rafe MacLaren's oldest son until Kade showed up." Javé didn't flinch when Mitch took a step toward him. "Ah, I've hit a nerve." He glanced at the woman behind Mitch. "Señora Dana MacLaren, sí?" Leaning forward, he lowered his voice. "Muy bonita, querida."

Mitch stepped forward, shoving Javé away. "Stay away from her."

Chuckling, he moved to a group of men. "Trey MacLaren. I believe the correct title is Naval Aviator, sí?"

Shifting, he looked at Matt. "My men tell me you are rodeo champion. Is this true?" He smirked when Matt remained silent, fisting his hands at his sides.

Looking at the man beside Matt, Javé took a step closer. "Cameron Sinclair. Señora MacLaren's oldest son. You will be giving her a grandchild soon."

Cam's nostrils flared, Matt's hard grip on his arm the only thing restraining him from slugging Javé.

He looked at Paige, nodded, then moved on.

Javé walked up to the last of the group. "Gage Templeton. You are with Double Ace. The woman beside you is Skye MacLaren, one of Rafe's daughters. I understand you are to be married in a few weeks, sí?"

Gage's hands balled into fists, a muscle in his jaw twitching as he worked to stop his instinct to grab the man by the throat and squeeze.

Turning back toward his club, Javé spread his arms out. "It's a good day for a long ride, amigos."

The men climbed back on their bikes. After taking one last, lingering look over his shoulder, Javé laughed before hitting the highway.

"Sonofabitch." Nesto's fist slammed into the palm of his other hand, his stomach churning. Sucking in a deep breath, he felt Kade's hand on his shoulder.

"Don't let him get to you, bro. We can handle this." Turning to the others, he walked up to them. "Javé is trying to intimidate us."

"He's doing a damn fine job of it." Mitch wrapped an arm around Dana's waist, pulling her close.

Nesto moved to Paige, settling his hands on her shoulders. "Are you all right?"

She let out a slow, shaky breath. "More angry than anything."

"I know the feeling." He glanced behind him, still hearing the rumble of the retreating bikes.

"We have to get them to stop, Nesto. What they're doing isn't right."

"I know, sweetheart. We'll talk to Paul on Monday, then set up a meeting between Jace and Javé. We'll have more to go on after they talk." Wrapping his arms around her, he kissed her forehead, then leaned back, staring into her eyes. "I'll keep you safe, Paige. You know that, right?"

Moving out of his embrace, she slid a hand down Rascal's neck. "I don't need you to protect me, Nesto."

Stepping behind her, he rested his hands on her hips. "What *do* you need?"

"For you to protect yourself and the others. The thought of losing you, or anyone else..." She swallowed twice, trying to dislodge the knot in her throat.

"Paige, don't do this to yourself." Turning her around to face him, he lifted her chin with his finger. "Listen to me. The MacLarens were a target before you took the job. I've already told you about what happened with Double Ace a few months ago. This is a continuation of the cartel trying to exert enough pressure on the family to turn over a legitimate operation for use in their illegal activities. It would've happened whether you came to Fire Mountain or not. Yes, Paul gave them your name, but even if he hadn't, Javé would've identified someone else to be the go-between. You heard him. He knows each one of us, our backgrounds, and who's important to us. At this point, you could leave and nothing would change." His gaze narrowed. "Perhaps that's what would be best."

Her brows furrowed. "What?"

"For you to leave, find a job somewhere else, and get as far away from this mess as possible. No one would blame you if you left. This is going to play out with the Sons whether you're here or not." It was an easy option, yet he didn't like voicing it. The last thing he wanted was for Paige to leave, kill any future for them. At the same time, he didn't want her blaming herself if someone got hurt, or worse.

Her chest tightened, mind reeling. Nesto wanted her gone and she hadn't seen it coming. After the last few days, she'd convinced herself they might have a second chance. What he suggested told her something else. Clearing her throat, she moved away at the same time Kade shouted for everyone to mount up.

"We'd better go." Grabbing Rascal's reins, she placed her left foot in the stirrup, swinging up and into the saddle.

"Paige..." He stood next to the horse, looking up at her.

"I'll consider the suggestion. The thing is, all you had to do was tell me we were over. You didn't need an elaborate excuse." Reining Rascal around, she moved next to Dana, ignoring Nesto as he called her name.

Chapter Fourteen

They'd ridden back to find a banquet prepared by the women who hadn't been with them. Paige had declined Nesto's help, insisting on removing the saddle and bridle herself. Afterward, she mimicked Sean's motions as he groomed his horse, then let him out into the large corral behind the barn.

The instant she walked through the front door, Brooke came up, a bright smile on her face. "Guess who called me trying to find you?"

Paige's stomach fell, thinking of Paul. "Who?"

"Your mother. She was just about to board a flight for Phoenix. It's good news, right?"

A relieved grin replaced the cautious expression. Reaching out, she gave Brooke a hug. "It's great news. I can't believe she found the courage to come without my father." Stepping back, she glanced over Brooke's shoulder. "I should find Annie, ask if she has recommendations for where my mother can stay while she's here."

"Already done. Annie offered a bedroom upstairs. Since J.D. and Clive are staying in your cabin, there are a couple extra rooms. Perfect timing."

"Hey, beautiful." Kade grabbed Brooke, giving her a kiss that wasn't sweet or quick.

Putting her hands on his chest, she pushed away, laughing. "Kade, the family may be watching."

"Let them." He bent her at the waist, kissing her again.

"Okay, I'm leaving you two in favor of a cold bottle of water." Seeing Annie standing alone, Paige moved around everyone to get to her. "Thank you for offering my mother a place to stay. I don't know how long she plans to be here, but as soon as J.D. and Clive leave, she and I can move back into my cabin. I mean, if that's all right with you."

"As long as Nesto says it's all right."

"I don't mean any disrespect, Annie, but he has nothing to do with it."

"I'm afraid he does, Paige." Her voice had an edge to it. "Nesto's been tasked with keeping you safe until whatever is happening goes away. When it's over, if you still want to move out, you can use the cabin as long as you want."

Paige caught her lower lip between her teeth, nodding. "You're right. It's just…"

"What, honey?"

Expelling a deep sigh, Paige clasped her hands in front of her. "Nesto's ready for me to be out from under him." She saw Annie's eyes widen, felt a presence behind her. Turning, she almost bumped into his chest.

"Excuse us, Annie, but Paige and I need to talk."

"Nesto, I don't think now is the time."

"Now is a great time. Come on." Gently gripping her arm, he led her to the back of the house and into the family room. Guiding her to the sofa, he motioned for her to sit down, then sat next to her.

She sat back, crossing her arms. "All right, spit it out so I can get something to drink."

Standing, he walked to the undercounter refrigerator, pulling out two bottles of water. Returning, he handed her one as he sat back down.

"Thanks."

Screwing off the cap, Nesto took a long swallow, not taking his eyes off Paige.

"What is it you want to say?"

He reached for her hand, relieved she didn't pull away. "Paul has put you in a terrible position. The fact you have no control over what's happening and other people are being affected is eating you up. The concern you have for others is one of the reasons I love you." He saw her eyes widen, heard her sharp intake of breath. "Look, I don't know whether you and I are going to work out, but I don't like seeing you hurt. You need to know there's an option to leave. It doesn't mean it's the choice I want you to make." Leaning forward, he stroked her cheek with back of his hand before brushing his lips across hers.

Reaching up, Paige cupped his face as he deepened the kiss, moaning when his arm went around her waist to drag her to him.

"Sorry to break this up, you two, but the food is being served."

Drawing back, Nesto rested his forehead against hers, chuckling. "Count on Sean to ruin the moment." Standing, he held out his hand, helping her up. "Ready to join the others?"

"Almost."

"Almost?" Nesto looked at her.

"Thank you for what you said. It means a lot after I thought you wanted me gone."

"I don't."

"Then you need to know I wasn't going to leave, although I did ask Annie about moving back to my cabin when Clive and J.D. leave."

Nesto shook his head. "Not going to happen."

"I mean when the threat is over."

He kissed her neck. "Still not going to happen."

"Nesto..."

"We're going to figure this out, but we're going to be together while we do it." He clasped her hand as he led her back to the kitchen.

"But—"

He placed a finger over her lips. "I need you with me as we figure this out, Paige. Please don't leave."

Leaning up, she kissed his cheek before turning to leave. A few steps later, she glanced over her shoulder, giving him a smug smile.

"I won't leave, but you may have to put up with my mother."

The sound of Nesto's laughter wafting outside brought a smile to Paige's face. To his credit, he hadn't balked at the possibility of having her mother in the guest room of his cabin. Although he attempted to hide it, the news she'd be staying with Annie and Heath brought an audible sigh of relief.

After everyone sat down to eat, Heath made the announcement there'd be no discussing the issues with Devil's Sons. Talking about the acquisitions was all right, the other clearly off limits.

"I hear you'll be working with me and the team on the review of Serenity." Sean tipped up his bottle of beer, taking a drink, looking at Paige.

"That's right, and I'm ready to start whenever you are. We've got until Friday to come up with a recommendation."

"First thing Monday morning would be great." Sean glanced up. "Looks like they're bringing out dessert. See you inside, Paige."

She watched Sean take a direct path to the table laden with a couple pies, cookies, and brownies, certain she couldn't put any more food in her stomach.

Brooke walked outside, motioning to her. "Your mother's here. She's in Heath's office."

Hurrying inside, Paige dashed into the den, spotting Annie talking to her mother. "Mother. I'm so glad you're here."

"I'll leave you two alone."

Paige didn't notice Annie leave as she hugged her mother, then stepped back, studying her face. Irene Wallace had always been a pretty woman with a slim figure, auburn hair, and ready smile. Her laughter brightened everyone's day. By the time Paige left Philadelphia, her clear complexion had dulled, she'd lost weight, and her hair had lost its shine.

"Have you had anything to eat?"

"I was too nervous about the trip to eat this morning, and all they had on the plane were peanuts and pretzels. The peanuts were honey-coated, though." Irene's weary smile told Paige all she needed to know.

"Come on. There's plenty of leftover food, whatever you want to drink, and a table full of desserts."

Irene shook her head. "I don't know, Paige. I'm not sure I can eat anything."

"After a day without food?" She slipped an arm through her mother's, urging her toward the kitchen.

"I don't know anyone."

"You know Ernesto and Brooke. Did I tell you she's pregnant?"

Her mother stopped walking. "Are you and Ernesto back together?"

"We are, Mrs. Wallace." Nesto walked up, kissing Irene on the cheek. "It's good to see you."

"You're looking well, Ernesto. Ranch life must agree with you."

He held back a chuckle, looking past Irene to lock his gaze on Paige. "That it does. I'll bet you haven't eaten. Let's go rustle you up some food."

"Rustle?" Irene mumbled, but didn't resist as they walked into a room filled with people she'd never met.

Paige looked at her mother. "See, there's plenty." Nesto filled her a plate with chicken, salad, and grilled vegetables while Paige made a couple introductions.

"Mother, this is Reyna and Caroline MacLaren. Reyna and Caroline, this is my mother, Irene Wallace. I'll be right back."

Caroline held out her hand, taking Irene's. "It's a pleasure. We'll all have lunch while you're in town. If you'll excuse me, I'm supposed to call my son, Blake." Hugging Reyna, she pulled out her phone, disappearing down the hall.

"It's wonderful to meet you." Reyna grasped Irene's hand in both of hers. "Paige is a wonderful girl, and Nesto is like a son to me. He and my son, Kade, grew up together."

"I haven't had a chance to meet Kade, but Brooke has been a good friend to Paige for years."

"Kade and Brooke are perfect for each other, the same as Nesto and Paige. I do hope those two can work out their problems and make a life. I love them both."

"Here you are, Mrs. Wallace." Nesto set the plate down. "Would you like some coffee?"

"Not now, Ernesto, but thank you. This looks wonderful."

Paige handed her a glass of water, then sat down next to her mother.

"I'll be with Kade if you need me." Nesto kissed Paige's forehead and hugged Reyna before walking away.

Irene picked at her food, her movements slow, as Paige and Reyna talked about the ranch and sights to see around Fire Mountain. After a while, she set down her fork, doing her best not to let depression overtake her.

"How's Father?"

Irene stiffened, moisture pooling in her eyes. Drawing from years of burying her feelings, schooling herself to hide emotions, she cleared her throat and glanced at Reyna.

"I should find Rafe."

Irene touched her arm. "No, Reyna. Stay. Please." When she sat back down, Irene glanced at Paige. "I'm sure your father is doing fine. He left early this week for Europe—with his mistress." She choked out the last, clutching her hands so tight her knuckles turned white.

Paige put an arm around her. "I'm so sorry, Mother."

"After all these years, everything we've been through, he chooses another woman." She swiped at a tear she'd been unable to contain. "I remember the last time we were in the Caribbean. It was a wonderful week. Peter must have told me a hundred times how much he loved me. Now it's as if it never happened."

Reyna took her hand, squeezing it. "You can stay here as long as you want. There's plenty of room, and you'll be with Paige."

"She's right, Mother. Don't go back."

Irene glanced between the two, a sad but genuine smile curling up the corners of her mouth. "I'm so glad you've offered. Before Peter got on the plane, I had him served with divorce papers."

Paige lay in Nesto's arms, his hand stroking her back, exhausted from his complete attention for over an hour. She knew they still had a long way to go, but something had changed between them.

"Are you tired?" Nesto kissed her head, pulling her closer.

"Bushed, but not sleepy. Why?"

"Don't take this wrong, sweetheart, but your father is a total bastard."

She choked out a laugh. "Odd. I was thinking the same. I'm so glad Mother decided to file for divorce and come out here. I'm hoping she'll stay."

"You don't want them to reconcile?"

She sighed. "When I first learned about his affair, yes, I hoped they'd work things out. When he continued seeing the other woman, I watched as the mother who raised me slipped away. The joy left her life, along with her spirit, and determination to love Father no matter what. Then she spotted them together. The woman is *my* age, Nesto.

Works in his office. No husband, children, or responsibilities outside of work. I've known Father's assistant most of my life. She didn't want to be disloyal to him, but she felt horrible for Mother. She confirmed they'd been seeing each other for months. God forgive me, but by the time I left Philadelphia, I hated him for what he'd done to her. Now all I feel is relief she's decided to get out of an ugly situation."

"Your mother is a good woman. She doesn't deserve what he's putting her through."

Paige rested a hand on his bare chest, glancing up at him. "You don't think he deserves a second chance?"

He knew her question applied to more than her mother and father. "What's going on with your parents can't be compared to what we're working through. Neither of us cheated." He thought of the women he'd been with since Paige left, feeling a spark of guilt, even though they weren't together. "From what your mother has said, he has no desire to give their marriage another chance. You and I want to make this relationship work, move beyond what happened between us."

Letting out a breath, he confronted his own part in her leaving. "It was my fault, too, Paige. I gave you no reason to believe you could come to me about problems with Paul. He'd burned too many bridges with me, used your generous nature for his own selfish reasons. Frankly, I was over his bull and manipulation. I also knew how much you loved him and your parents. Without knowing it, my actions forced you to make a choice."

"And now we're here," she breathed out.

"Yes, we're here, which isn't a bad place to be." Lowering his head, he kissed her, groaning when Paige rolled on top of him, straddling his waist. Reaching up, he threaded his fingers through her hair, drawing her back down to within an inch of his mouth. "I love you, Paige."

"And I love you, Nesto."

Chapter Fifteen

"Are you certain you want to look for a place to live in Fire Mountain, Mother? You haven't been here a full day yet." Paige sat outside the cabin, Irene next to her, each enjoying hot cups of coffee in the clear Sunday morning air.

Irene had driven her rental car to Nesto's cabin early, unable to stay in bed, images of her husband ruining all her quiet moments.

Holding the cup with both hands, Irene took a sip. "I've already given it a great deal of thought, Paige. My life is no longer in Philadelphia where I could run into your father and his..." Her voice faltered before she continued. "Our *friends* know what your father has done. Most have chosen to ignore it, as if it isn't an issue." She glanced at Paige, her eyes haunted. "The women I thought were my friends seldom call. I'm the one being pushed out because they all perceive your father as the one with the money."

Paige thought of her mother's enormous trust fund, knowing her father had no access to it. The assets accumulated during the marriage would most likely be split between them, making her mother far richer than her father. On top of that, he might even be ordered to pay alimony since her mother had never worked. Paige hated the thought, but right now, she didn't feel a bit of sympathy for him.

"As you know, I have my own funds, separate from your father's. I don't need much. Two or three bedrooms, two bathrooms." Irene looked over the valley at the mountains. "A view would be lovely."

Paige shook her head, chuckling. "Mother, you could afford to buy a good portion of the town. I'm sure you'll find something suitable."

"No, Paige. You don't understand. I don't want a showpiece, anything ostentatious. Something like this cabin, maybe a little larger, would be wonderful—and it would be *mine*."

"Ladies." Nesto walked outside holding a pot of coffee and tray with cream and sugar. "Refills?" He set the tray on the table before leaning down to give Paige a kiss.

"Thank you, Ernesto." Irene held up her cup.

He filled both cups, seeing Clive and J.D. emerge from Paige's cabin. "Excuse me, ladies." Setting down the pot, Nesto walked over to meet them. "What do you boys have planned today?"

"Do you have a minute to come inside?" Clive asked.

Nesto nodded, following them into the cabin. "What's going on?" He walked to the fireplace, turned toward them, and crossed his arms.

J.D. sat on the arm of the sofa. "I'll let Clive tell you what we know."

"I can't tell you much, but we have some new information on Devil's Sons and their association with Satan's Brethren."

"What can you tell me?" Nesto dropped his arms, taking a seat in a nearby chair.

"The DEA has information on the Brethren that could bring them down."

"Have you told, Kade?"

Clive shook his head. "Not yet. We've been tasked with a couple meetings today. We'll know more afterward. The problem is the boss isn't too interested in sharing information with anyone outside the agency. We'll tell you what we can, but it may not be much."

"Understood. We'll take whatever you can share."

"J.D. and I will be back before dinner. We'll plan to meet with you and Kade here at the cabin."

Nesto stood, walking to the door. "I'll let Kade know."

Heading back to the cabin, he couldn't help wondering what new information they had on Satan's Brethren, a club into gunrunning, prostitution, drugs. He didn't believe they had their hands in human trafficking, but their founder, Sonny Morgan, and his son, Robbie, weren't adverse to any illegal activity, as long as it brought in a lot of cash.

Their ties to Devil's Sons, a club requiring all members to prove their Hispanic blood, had surprised those in the DEA. The two had been at war for years. After Robbie helped strike a deal, the two gangs had gotten along relatively well.

Opening the door to his cabin, Nesto stepped inside, spotting Paige in the kitchen, Irene leaning against the counter.

"How about breakfast?" Paige looked down at what she had on the counter, then took stock of the ingredients in the cupboards. "Pancakes, eggs, and bacon sound good?"

A grin split his face. "Are you cooking?"

She placed her hands on her hips, raising a brow. "Is that a problem?"

Holding up his hands, he took a couple steps backward. "Not at all. I'll set out the plates."

Paige sat behind the wheel of her mother's rental, Irene in the passenger seat as they toured Fire Mountain. They'd visited three open houses with four more still on their list.

"I think this next one might be exactly what I'm looking for."

Paige looked out the corner of her eye at her mother. "That's what you said about the last one."

"The pictures must have been altered to make the rooms look larger." Irene crinkled her nose. "The next one looks somewhat like Nesto's cabin. Very quaint with a fireplace, garage, and view. I can pay cash for it."

"Mother, you can pay cash for almost any house in town. Look for one you love, in good condition, in a nice neighborhood."

They made a few more turns before Irene pointed to the For Sale sign. "It's right up ahead."

Paige pulled to a stop, looking across her mother and out the passenger window. "It's beautiful." Turning off the engine, she grabbed her purse. "Let's look inside."

Irene took a flyer from a box on the sign, reading through it as they continued up the walkway. "Everything matches what we saw in the internet posting."

"Please, come inside." A professionally dressed woman, who appeared to be in her late forties or early fifties, stood in the doorway, offering them a warm smile. "I'm Helen Henry, the agent for the seller."

Paige and Irene introduced themselves, then stepped inside. They came to an abrupt halt when they saw the view.

Helen laughed. "Everyone has the same reaction. The home has an unobstructed view of Fire Mountain. The lot is over half an acre. Three bedrooms, three bathrooms, an updated kitchen, and a smaller room the current owners use as an office." She looked at Irene. "Do you work?"

She shook her head. "No, but I have an idea of what I want to do. I just need the right home in the right town."

Paige took a step away, cocking her head as she stared at her mother. Irene grinned when she saw the confused look on her daughter's face.

"I've always had dreams, Paige. There are things I've wanted to do, but never had time with all of your father's commitments." Irene looked at Helen. "May we look around?"

"Please." She gestured with her arm. "Take your time. When you're finished, feel free to ask me any questions. If I don't have an answer, I'll get one for you."

Irene walked toward the kitchen, her gaze taking in the pine cabinets, granite countertops, and expensive appliances. The windowed breakfast nook continued the view from Fire Mountain north. The yard was small by her standards, but much larger than she hoped to find so close to downtown. Paige stepped next to her.

"This is very nice, Mother. The original town is three blocks away."

Moving through the rest of the house, they made a few comments, then took a walk in the back yard, ending up in the living room with Helen.

"What do you think?"

Irene hesitated a moment before tilting her head. "It's lovely. The kitchen is stunning, but the bathrooms need updating. I do like the entry from the garage into the kitchen, and the large fireplace."

Helen picked up a piece of paper, writing down Irene's comments. "The owners know the bathrooms need some work, but they have taken that into account in the listing price."

Irene pulled the listing from her purse, reviewing the details. "The house three blocks over is a similar size with a view and is thirty thousand dollars less."

Helen stepped up next to her. "If you're referring to the house on Weber, it's ten years older with only a partial kitchen remodel. And, in my opinion, this is a nicer neighborhood."

"Perhaps." Irene took one more look around, then extended her hand. "It was a pleasure meeting you, Helen. I'll need to think about it."

Pulling cards from her pocket, she handed one to Irene, the other to Paige. "Do you have an agent?"

Irene glanced at Paige, who shook her head. "Not yet."

"Tell you what. Look at some other houses, think about it, and if you want to make an offer, I'd be glad to write it up for you. I'm able to work with both the seller and buyer, but can call in another agent if a conflict of interest arises."

Irene nodded. "Thank you. I'll consider it."

Paige followed her mother outside and into the car, reconciling the broken woman who arrived last night to the strong, confident woman of today. An amazing transition in twenty-four hours. Driving away, she glanced at her mother.

"Did you like it?"

"I adored it." Irene couldn't wipe the smile from her face.

"Then why didn't you make an offer?"

"Because buying property is like poker, honey. She knows I like the home and is also aware I think it's overpriced. She'll talk to the owners. By the time I call Helen in a couple days, they'll be ready for a lower offer."

"What if it sells? It seems the perfect house for you." Paige continued to the next house on their list.

Irene grew quiet, then let out a slow breath. "I thought your father was perfect, too. I'm learning there's no perfect house and certainly no perfect husband. If this house sells, I'll find another. Or buy a piece of land and build my own. I'm an independent woman now, Paige. Like you, I have all kinds of options available to me."

The last open houses didn't compare to the one Irene loved the minute she stepped inside. Paige respected her mother's opinion, feeling a surge of pride in the way she handled herself. Then again, she'd had years of practice moderating her behavior to appease her husband. Add to that all the times she'd negotiated with caterers, entertainers, and venues for the large fundraisers she'd chaired over the years. The thought triggered a question she hadn't asked earlier.

"Mother, you told Helen you had dreams, things you still wanted to do. What are they?"

"I've so many, it's hard to pick a couple." Sighing, Irene glanced out the window as they pulled to a stop in front of the cabin.

Paige killed the engine, making no move to open the door. "Tell me one. When you're ready, you can share the others."

"Do you know I have a degree in business?"

Eyes wide, Paige leaned forward. "I never knew you attended college at all."

Irene continued to stare out the window. "I met your father in college. Thank goodness I had only a few credits to complete or I may have dropped out to marry him. He stole my heart on our first date. Within a month, we were engaged. The Saturday after graduation, we married, then moved into a one bedroom apartment on campus so he could complete his master's." She glanced over at Paige. "He didn't want me to work. Said he needed my support, which would be a full-time job. He was right. Now I'm fifty-two, will soon be divorced, and my one and only job was working in the college bookstore. I'm not sure how I'll do it, but I'm determined to make it on my own."

"You'll never want for anything, Mother, so I'm certain this isn't about money."

"It's about a new beginning. I'm excited, but also scared."

Paige reached over, taking her mother's hand. "I'm here for you, and so is Nesto. In fact, I guarantee you can count on every person on this ranch. Are you sure you want a home of your own? I know the MacLarens would find a place for you here."

"Other than making the decision to leave your father, I've never been more certain of anything in my life."

"What is your gut feeling on this, Clive?" Kade leaned forward, resting his arms on his legs.

"You know I can't tell you what's in the works. What I can say is Robbie is in deep. He runs the chapters west of

Texas. His father, Sonny, is still the national president. Right now, what the agency has points to Robbie and his club." He looked at Kade. "I know you and he were close when you were undercover."

Kade snorted. "As close as a cop can get to a thug like Robbie. I saw goodness and pure evil in the man. He was older, had his own tight circle, but I did learn a lot about him, including his desire to forge an alliance with Devil's Sons. I heard it had happened, and wondered how long until it blew up."

J.D. took a sip of beer, then leaned back in his chair. "That's where it gets interesting. You already know Clive and I had a couple meetings today. Can't tell you who was involved, but from what we learned, Satan's Brethren hasn't learned the extent of Javé's latest adventures."

"How can that be?" Nesto asked. "It isn't as if Javé and his club have been subtle. They ride the roads as if they own them. Flaunt what they do, acting as if they're above it all. How could this not get back to the Brethren?"

"I didn't say the Brethren don't know anything. They just may not be aware of what Javé's trying to pull off with the MacLarens." J.D. tossed down a folder.

Kade opened it as Nesto moved next to him to scan the pages, then set the file down. After a few minutes, they glanced at each other before looking at Clive and J.D.

"The information in that folder doesn't leave this room. It's all you're going to get, so don't even think of asking for more." Leaning down, J.D. scooped up the file, tossing it into his open case. "There's more, but you've seen the basics."

Nesto leaned back against the sofa. "It's enough to put a huge hole in the Brethren's business."

Clive nodded. "Yeah, but the boss wants to bring down the Sons and the Montalvo-Ortiz cartel."

"He's using the Brethren," Kade mumbled, referring to the man who used to be his boss.

Neither Clive nor J.D. responded.

Standing, Nesto moved toward the door. "I expect Paige to hear from Paul or Javé tomorrow about the meeting. At least we know our guess about what the Sons are after is close."

Kade stood, moving next to Nesto. "Too close."

Chapter Sixteen

"It's confirmed. Jace and I will meet with Javé this evening. Here's the address. Do you know it?"

Nesto handed the information to Heath, who nodded.

"It's an abandoned property we own on the old highway about twenty minutes from here." Heath cast a concerned gaze at Jace. "I don't like this. I thought he'd want to meet at a park, not some remote place."

"It's typical for a meeting like this one, Heath. Nesto will be with Jace. J.D., Clive, and I will be positioned around the location. Remember, Javé wants this to work. He needs the Double Ace distribution network to move the product, so he'll make certain whoever he brings with him doesn't lay a hand on either of them." Kade hoped to reassure him, as well as Jace.

"Do you want to go over the specifics, Kade?" Nesto asked.

Nodding, Kade turned his gaze on Jace. "You'll leave your phone behind. Expect them to pat you and Nesto down. They'll do their best to intimidate you before, during, and after the meeting. Expect him to have his VP stay in the room, maybe his sergeant-at-arms. Don't let them bother you. It's all part of the game. Listen to what they want, ask the same questions you'd ask in any business meeting. No matter what Javé says, don't let him get to you. Paige wore a wire in the bar with Paul. Totally unsanctioned and useless for anything other than having other ears on what Paul said. Since this is off the record, as far as the DEA is concerned, there'll be no wires in this meeting. They'll find them when they search you anyway. I'd expect everything to take no more than thirty minutes. Any questions?"

"None. I'm ready to get this behind us."

Kade clasped him on the shoulder. "We all are, Uncle Jace."

Paige toyed with her food in the café a few miles from the office, unable to summon up an appetite, even as her stomach growled.

"Are you going to just stare at your salad?" Nesto picked up his soda, took a swallow, then set the can down.

She didn't answer, picking up a forkful of food, then setting it back down. "I'm worried about the meeting."

Reaching across the table, Nesto settled his hand over hers. "There's no reason for it. Javé isn't going to harm Jace or me. There's too much riding on him working out a deal with the MacLarens."

"How can you be sure?"

"There are never any guarantees, especially when dealing with men such as Javé." Removing his hand from on top of hers, he crossed his arms. "You'll have to decide whether or not you can trust me on this, Paige. If you can't, there's nothing more I can say. Maybe you should discuss this with Kade."

"I didn't mean—"

His gaze narrowed, his stomach churning at her lack of faith. "Yes, you did. We talked about this last week, last night, and this morning. Now you're questioning me again." Memories flashed in his head. Standing, he nodded toward the door. "If you're finished, we should get back to the office. I'll wait for you in the truck."

Paige watched him walk out, working to control the knot of pain threatening to choke her. He was right, and not just about today. Back in San Diego, she would question everything. It drove Nesto crazy, causing a lot of stress for both of them, until she'd let her lack of faith in him destroy the relationship. She didn't want that to happen again. They had a second chance and she meant for it to work. Unless she came clean, told him her fears, the doubts plaguing her, they wouldn't make it.

Grabbing her purse, she sucked in a deep breath to bolster her courage. Nesto sat in his truck, his hands gripping the steering wheel, gaze focused straight ahead. Tugging at her lower lip, she climbed into the passenger seat, clasping her hands together.

"When do you need to get back?"

Nesto didn't look at her. "No later than two."

"Same here. We have a little time. Do you feel like taking a drive?"

"I've got a lot on my mind, Paige. Now isn't a good time."

"It's important, Nesto."

She watched his jaw tighten, his throat work before he turned to face her, resting his arm across the back of the seat.

"If you've got something to say, just say it."

Paige didn't want to discuss this in the parking lot of the café. Fire Mountain was a small town, MacLaren Enterprises the biggest employer. Anyone they knew could walk by, see them inside his truck. When she didn't answer, he turned away, meaning to start the engine.

"Wait." Reaching toward him, she gripped his arm. When he remained silent, she squeezed, leaning forward. "Please."

Letting out a frustrated breath, he sat back. "Fine. Talk to me."

Paige knew this would be hard. She just didn't expect to fight nausea and the tightening of her chest. "It's my fault."

Turning toward her, he cocked his head, doing his best to keep the disdain from his voice. "What exactly is your fault?"

"It started a couple years after we started dating."

Confusion clouded his expression. "What started?"

"When I began having doubts about you...about us. You'd be late to pick me up, cancel at random times, not call when you told me you would. I began to wonder what was going on."

His face softened. "Paige, you always knew my job could be unpredictable. Assignments came up with little notice, meetings went longer than intended. I never lied to you about what was going on. Not once."

Rubbing her temples, she expelled a shaky breath. "I know you didn't. It's just, well...I found things sometimes."

"You'll have to be more specific."

"Initials, phone numbers on pieces of paper you left on the kitchen counter or the dresser."

"Paige, if I were trying to hide something from you, I sure as hell wouldn't have left the evidence right in front of you." The anger in his voice had her leaning back, even though she knew he'd never hurt her.

"I know...I know. You even explained they had to do with your work." Closing her eyes, she forced the rest out. "I loved you, trusted you, but I couldn't help myself from having doubts. Then I ran into you at the café near my apartment having coffee with a woman I'd never met and you wouldn't introduce her. Afterward, you refused to tell me anything about her."

Nesto rubbed the back of his neck. "I remember. She was from another agency. We were on a joint task force and she wanted to speak with me privately." He glanced up, noting the wary look in Paige's eyes. "I should've explained it to you at the time, but I thought you'd jump to conclusions."

"And now?"

"Membership on the task force was classified, but there was another reason I didn't introduce you."

Her stomach churned at the look on his face. One telling her he'd never intended to share this information. "Tell me."

"She and I went out for over a year. It ended before I met you, so I never talked about her. That day, she'd asked if we could try again, start where we'd left off." Paige's quick intake of breath had him reaching across the seat to grasp her hand. "I told her I had no interest in seeing her again and was in a serious relationship. That was the end of it. She never brought it up again." He tightened his grip on her hand, studying her face. "There were no other women after I met you."

Paige relaxed against the seat, her mouth tipping into a grim smile. "I believe you." She placed a hand on her chest. "In my heart, I always knew I could trust you."

"But your head didn't agree."

"No," she snorted. "My doubts started after I saw my father with another woman when I visited. It was long before Mother knew about his affair, and over a year before they asked me to help with Paul. I don't know if it's the same woman he's seeing now, and it doesn't matter. The point is, I saw him leave a restaurant with her. They walked together, holding hands, kissing. Then they walked into a nearby hotel, registered, and got on the elevator." Paige looked up at Nesto, her father's betrayal obvious on her face. "I ran through the lobby into the ladies' room and got sick. It made me physically ill to see him with someone else. I can't imagine how it would've affected my mother. I chose not to tell her. It happened a couple weeks after I saw you with that woman."

Mumbling a curse, he shook his head. "Why didn't you tell me? We could've talked about it."

Shaking her head, she covered his hand with hers. "I know that now, but at the time, I couldn't shake the feeling you were hiding something from me. No matter how much I told myself you'd never do what my father did, I couldn't purge the notion from my mind. Months went by, your work had you traveling almost every week. We were growing apart and I didn't know what to do to change it. When my parents called, it only took my mother's crying to get me on the plane." Her eyes gleamed with moisture. "I'm so sorry, Nesto. I never should've let my doubts rule what I did." Groaning, she swiped at a tear she hadn't been able to contain.

He didn't know what to say. She'd struggled with trust far longer than he realized, triggered by his determination not to discuss his ex-lover and Paige's knowledge her father was cheating. Communication had been the characteristic of their relationship he'd valued most. They could talk about any subject, be honest in their thoughts, knowing the other wouldn't judge them. At some point, it all fell apart, and he hadn't realized it.

"You should've said something, Paige. We could've worked this out long ago." Pulling his hand away, he started the truck, driving straight to the office.

"They're here." Nesto nodded toward the sound of motorcycles coming toward them. "We'll know what Javé wants soon, Jace."

Crossing his arms, Jace planted his feet shoulder width apart, watching the Devil's Sons approach. He counted six bikes, his gaze moving to the locations he knew Kade, Clive, and J.D. waited. His Ruger 22, tucked in the waistband of his pants, would've given him added comfort. Unfortunately, it lay hidden in his truck in the office parking lot.

Nesto hadn't said any more since spotting the club riding toward them, remaining silent as Javé, his vice president, and sergeant-at-arms parked their bikes and closed the distance between them.

Nesto didn't wait for Javé to speak. "Let's get inside before anyone sees us."

"Introductions first." Javé smiled, holding out his hand. "Javé Cruz, president of the Devil's Sons."

Jace looked at the outstretched hand, but didn't take it. "Jace MacLaren."

"One more thing, I'm afraid." Javé nodded at his men, who walked up to Jace and Nesto. "You don't mind if my men check for weapons."

Raising their arms, Nesto and Jace said nothing as they were checked. When his men stepped away, Nesto moved toward them.

"Our turn." Their eyes narrowed, but at Javé's nod, they allowed Nesto to pat them down. He did it with the thoroughness he'd learned from years as a marshal. When he'd checked all three, he stepped back.

Jace stepped toward the building. "Let's do what Mr. Salgado suggested and go inside."

Chuckling, Javé turned to his two men, stretching out his arms, and shrugged. "We are to follow *Mr. Salgado*." His vice president smiled, lifting a chin to the other three club members who would stay with the bikes.

Opening the door, Nesto walked inside first, looking for threats. Seeing none, he motioned Jace forward. Once everyone entered, he shut the door. He and Jace took a position on one side of an imaginary line, while Javé and his men stayed on the other.

Jace took the lead, focusing his gaze on Javé. "We're here. Tell us what you want."

"Right to the point. I like that," Javé said, his voice holding a tinge of scorn. "It is simple. I run a business and need a new method of distributing our products. I understand you plan to purchase Double Ace. Their location and operation suit our needs. We want to offer you a lucrative contract. You carry our products to destinations we provide, and MacLaren Enterprises makes a sizable profit. You, Jace MacLaren, are a businessman, the same as me. All businessmen seek new ways of making a profit, sí? The Sons are offering you an easy way to enrich your bottom line."

Jace narrowed his gaze on him. "What products would you be shipping?"

Javé shrugged. "It is of no importance as long you deliver what we provide and we deposit money into your account."

"The nature of the shipments will determine whether we even consider working for you, Mr. Cruz."

"Javé, please. We are friends, no?"

Jace didn't waver. "What products, *Javé*?"

The Sons' president took a step toward him, narrowing his gaze, his mouth set in a thin line. To his credit, Jace didn't budge, showing no signs of fear or the intimidation Javé desired.

"You and I should talk."

"We are talking."

"In private. Two businessmen working out details. I am certain we can come to some arrangement."

Jace turned to Nesto. "Excuse us for a minute." Gesturing for Javé to lead the way, they walked several paces from the others, turning their backs for privacy. "All right. We're alone. Tell me the details."

"You are a smart man with a family who loves you, depends on you to protect them. Your oldest son, Blake, is going to school at Montana State University, getting his master's. Your other son, Brett, is in college, too, although he is unsure if he'll stay where he is or change schools."

Jace's nostrils flared, his jaw set, forcing himself to stay calm.

"And Señora MacLaren—Caroline, sí? A beautiful woman who's stayed with you, even when you went to another woman." Javé chuckled, then held up his hands when Jace took a step forward. "It is nothing to me. My woman, she does not care when I take others to my bed. It is not the same for you. Your wife is not a happy woman." Javé shrugged. "But you already know this is true."

Temper flaring, Jace grabbed the collar of Javé's jacket, leaning into his face. "Are you making threats against my family? If you are, I promise, you will live to regret it."

He'd barely gotten the words out when Nesto and Javé's men ran forward. The vice president grasped Jace's arms, dragging him away while the sergeant-at-arms threw a punch at Nesto, who dodged it, landing his own blow to the man's jaw.

"Enough!" Javé shouted, looking at his men. "You will stay back."

Nesto looked at Jace, looking for any sign he wanted to leave, cut the meeting off. Jace shook his head. Nodding, Nesto backed away, making certain the other two club officers did the same.

Javé straightened his jacket, his anger barely under control. "I make no threats. I know much about all the MacLarens." Reaching into his pocket, he extracted a piece of paper, handing it to Jace.

His anger rose as Jace read the names of all family members and close friends, their addresses, phone numbers, ages, and where they hung out. It even included the surgery his son, Blake, had endured a few years earlier. An operation fewer than a dozen people knew about.

"There is more, but that is all you need to see." The smirk on Javé's face had Jace fisting his hands at his sides. "Do we have an agreement?"

Jace wanted to say *hell no*. Instead, he glanced at Nesto. "I'll have an answer for you next week."

"Three days."

"Sorry, Javé. It can't be done that soon. We haven't made a final decision to buy Double Ace. That won't happen for several more days."

Javé stepped to within several inches of Jace. "You will have an answer for me by Friday."

"And if I don't?"

Javé chuckled, his face twisting into a sneer. "Do you truly want to know?"

Chapter Seventeen

Nesto and Jace spent two hours debriefing Kade, J.D., Clive, Heath, and Rafe after the meeting with Javé. Kade wrote down every detail from both men's perspective, reviewing what they remembered several times, determined not to miss anything.

Heath couldn't stop reading over the paper Javé had handed Jace, the one containing what the club knew about his family and close friends. Blake's surgery caught his attention. The only way the information could've been obtained was to have someone working inside the hospital, or a talented hacker who could breach their computer system.

Scanning it again, Heath's gaze landed on Amber Sinclair, Eric's wife, his brow raising in surprise. Nothing indicated Javé knew who she was or her connection to Satan's Brethren. Another closely held secret of the MacLaren family. After what had happened to her, they'd vowed not to bring the Brethren, their founder, or their West Coast president up in conversation unless a critical situation arose. Tapping his finger on the paper, Heath cleared his throat.

"There's nothing next to Amber's name about Satan's Brethren."

Kade's eyes widened. "He may not have listed it, keeping it quiet to pull out and use later."

"Or he just doesn't know," Nesto said. "Could the agency have it in their files, Clive?"

"I know for a fact it's in Robbie's file because I had to include it. It's a sentence or two with no details about her. Even if Javé has someone inside the DEA, and that's highly doubtful, it would be almost impossible for them to sort through thousands of documents to find it."

Jace breathed a sigh of relief. "Well, if there's one piece of good news in all this mess, it's that the Sons don't know of the connection."

Nesto rubbed his chin, resting his arms on the table. "We're in a helluva situation here, gentlemen." He looked at Clive and J.D. "With what we know, can you go to your boss?"

Kade nodded, looking at Clive. "Does he have enough information to pull resources from other operations to focus on this?"

Clive and J.D. exchanged looks.

"What?" Rafe asked, seeing a look he couldn't define on the face of each agent.

J.D. clicked his pen a few times, blowing out a breath. "Perhaps, but it's doubtful. He knows Clive and I are here, helping with a supposed threat—on our own time. The agency is as understaffed now as before Kade left."

"What if he could bring down two clubs in one operation?"

All eyes shifted to Nesto.

"What do you have in mind, bro?" Kade leaned back in his chair, crossing his arms.

Nesto turned toward Kade. "Clive and J.D. showed us what they could about the DEA case against the Brethren. You and I know it's good, possibly air-tight, but with the way the courts work these days, who knows. My guess is the DEA and Justice Department are working a few angles, pitting members against each other, using informants, exaggerating what they've got in order to worry the club. My gut tells me the case may be a lot more bark than bite."

Kade looked at J.D., who shifted in his chair, and Clive, whose expression showed nothing. He knew Nesto didn't expect them to confirm or deny. "From what you boys didn't say, the agency has little on the Sons. What if you could go to your boss with a plan to use the Brethren to get to the Sons—and possibly their partners?"

Heath, Jace, and Rafe listened, not interrupting or asking questions, interested in the turn of the conversation.

Clive rubbed the back of his neck, moving his head from side to side. Standing, he paced a few feet from the table, glancing out at the darkening sky. Shoving his hands into his pockets, he turned to look at Heath, Jace, and Rafe.

"Special Agent in Charge Dennis Johnson, our boss and the man Kade once reported to, is a man who goes by the book. He'll look the other way from time to time, like with J.D. and me coming here to help out old friends. His team has worked for years using some of what Kade learned while undercover, unearthing new charges on the

Brethren." He looked at Nesto and Kade. "You two are going to need to come up with a solid argument. Personally, I think you're on the right track. Feed information to Satan's Brethren about what the Sons are doing with the cartel. When Robbie finds out Amber could be a target, I'd bet my next vacation the lid will blow. During the turmoil, we may even learn a little about Javé's other partners. What do you think, J.D.?"

"If we get the details sorted right, I'm willing to take it to Johnson."

Clive nodded. "I'll be right with you."

Nesto's face relaxed for the first time in hours. He looked at Heath. "If this is all right with you, Rafe, and Jace, I'd suggest Kade, J.D., Clive, and I get together early tomorrow to sort out what to present to Johnson. We'll run it by you before we go forward, but we need to get on this right away."

Heath stood and walked over to Nesto, clasping him on the shoulder. "Whatever you need to do to get Javé and his gang of thugs away from our family, we're behind you. Any resources you need, just ask."

The sun had set by the time Kade parked out front of the ranch house where Brooke and Paige waited for him and Nesto to take them to their cabins. Even the added security Nesto had set up didn't calm their apprehension concerning Javé.

Kade turned toward Nesto. "I think what we talked about tonight has a good chance to sway Johnson. He's not as hard-nosed as J.D. and Clive said, but he is cautious and requires a mountain of intel before making changes."

Nesto glanced at the front door, not ready to get out of the truck and face Paige. Learning she hadn't trusted him for months before she left San Diego weighed on him in a way he couldn't reconcile. She should've come to him, opened up about her concerns. Maybe she didn't because Paige knew he'd be honest. But she also should've known he'd never go behind her back, having an affair while they were a couple. It just wasn't something he could stomach. It was why he felt so much disgust at what her father had done to Irene.

"Hey, bro. Are you okay?"

Shaking his head, Nesto nodded. "I'm good, man. Just got a lot on my mind. We do need Satan's Brethren to go after Devil's Sons. You know Robbie better than anyone. Do you really believe he'll care enough to start a war if he learns Amber might be in danger?"

"Hard to tell. He never mentioned having a daughter the entire time I knew him—and we became pretty close."

Nesto shook his head. "What man doesn't want to protect his own daughter?"

"Well, now, that's the thing about the outlaw life. The club comes first in all things, even family. With her mother out of the picture, Robbie put Amber up for adoption a few years after her birth, when he accepted the outlaw life wouldn't allow him to be the parent she deserved. A man who didn't care wouldn't form a bond with his daughter, build a relationship, then walk away unless he had a damn good reason. Plus, he rode off again when they found each other after all those years. It about killed Amber, but she moved on and married Eric. Something about the way it all came down makes me think he'll bring the wrath of the entire Satan's Brethren organization down on Javé if he learns Amber is one of his targets."

"I hope you're right because we're betting a lot on it." Gripping the door handle, he took one more look at the house, as ready as he'd ever be to see Paige. "Guess we'd better go in and get our girls."

Climbing out of the truck, Nesto did his best to clear his head, rein in the reservations tormenting him after Paige's confession. He had no doubt she loved him. Too bad love alone wasn't enough.

"If you want, I can sleep in the guest room." Paige fiddled with the bottom edge of the t-shirt she wore at night, wishing Nesto would say something about their talk outside the café. Neither of them had spoken during the ride from the ranch house to his cabin, and he'd said little since closing the door.

Removing his pistol from its holster, setting it on the table next to the bed, he looked at her. "Is that what you want?"

"No."

"Good. Neither do I." He finished emptying his pockets, pulled his shirt over his head, and tossed it in a basket by the door. "I need some time to process what you said today." Walking to her, he rested his hands on her shoulders. "I've got to know you believe in me, Paige. Neither of us can have doubts about the other. Love isn't enough. We'll never make it unless there's trust between us." He didn't lean down to kiss her, stroke her hair, or do any of the things he did when being affectionate. Instead, he dropped his hands and left the room.

Following him into the kitchen, she leaned against the counter, watching his efficient movements as he prepared coffee for the following morning. She loved everything about him. His blatant sexuality, along with his confident nature without being a jerk, had been what drew her to him at first sight. It hadn't taken long to learn he had many layers. Paige found she enjoyed peeling away each one, discovering more reasons to love him each time.

"My uncertainties weren't your fault, Nesto. I've had a lot of time over the last two years to think about it, and it's all on me. I should've said something to you, forced you to tell me about the woman."

Crossing his arms, he settled a hip against the counter and snorted. "As if you could've forced me to do anything. My mistake was thinking I could ignore your questions about her. If it had been me, I would've been all kinds of crazy, wondering what was going on."

A slow grin appeared on her face. "You wouldn't have let it rest, and you know it. Me? I buried it all inside, afraid I'd lose you if I pushed."

Moving to stand in front of her, he ran his hands down her arms, then moved them up to grip the back of her head, spearing his fingers through her hair. Angling her head to the side, he captured her mouth with his in a slow, deep kiss. Pulling back, he rested his forehead against hers.

"We've got to work this out, babe."

"You sure you still want this, Nesto?"

He nodded, not loosening his hold on her. "It's what I've wanted since the day I met you."

Nesto woke before dawn, unable to get his mind off the meeting with Javé and the threats he'd made. Though not overt, they'd been threats all the same.

Jace told Javé a decision about buying Double Ace hadn't been made, which was a lie. If Javé suspected otherwise, he didn't let it show.

An informal agreement had been reached between Ivan Santiago, Gage Templeton, and the MacLarens—a purchase price established and an acquisition date identified. It was expected to move quickly, finalizing in thirty days if the attorneys acted fast. Javé didn't need to know this.

Shifting onto his side, he leaned down, brushing aside a strand of Paige's hair before kissing her cheek. He hoped last night could be a turning point for them.

Careful not to wake her, he slid from the bed, grabbed some clothes, and walked into the bathroom. He needed a shower to clear his head before meeting with the others to finalize their thoughts on approaching Special Agent in Charge Dennis Johnson.

Kade would be by any minute to pick him up and drop off Mitch, who'd drive Paige and Brooke to the office. Although Nesto didn't expect any trouble from Javé before the Friday deadline, he refused to leave the women unprotected.

Emerging from the bathroom, dressed, his hair still damp, he sat on the edge of the bed. Her face looked so serene, so beautiful, it made his heart ache. Stroking a hand down her arm, he waited as her eyes fluttered open. A slow smile spread across her face.

"Hey." She raised a hand, cupping his face.

Leaning down, he kissed her. "Kade will be here soon with Brooke and Mitch. He'll drive you to the office. How about meeting for lunch? I'll come by your office."

"Sounds good."

Standing, he looked down at her. "Don't go back to sleep, sweetheart. I'd hate for Mitch to see you in your pajamas."

She tossed off the covers, showcasing the fact she hadn't worn pajamas to bed. "Guess I shouldn't give him a shock." Standing, she rose on her toes, kissed him, then rushed to the bathroom, closing the door.

"Are we all agreed?" Kade looked at Nesto, Clive, and J.D. They'd been sequestered behind closed doors for hours, hammering out the final details of what the agents would present to their boss via conference call that afternoon.

Clive finished scribbling a few notes before looking up. "Only Johnson and his superiors know everything the agency has on Satan's Brethren. I've been told it's solid and could put some members away for years, including Robbie. We're asking them to take a chance on their case by alerting the Brethren of Javé's activities and threats. There's no telling what Robbie will do when he learns Amber is on the list of targets. Johnson may not be willing to take the risk."

"Even if it means protecting the MacLarens from Javé?" Nesto knew how it all worked, but he'd never liked how a lot of decisions were made in a bureaucracy as thick as a spider's web.

J.D. shrugged. "We won't know until we have our call this afternoon."

"What's your gut tell you?" Nesto scrubbed a hand down his face, needing some read on how the meeting would go.

Clive shook his head. "We have it all laid out for him. I think we have a good shot at getting him to pull some resources, make this happen. But don't quote me on that."

"Mother, Annie, and Reyna are looking at a few more houses today. If the one house hasn't sold, I'm pretty sure she'll make an offer on it." Paige took another bite of her sandwich, chewed, then swallowed before continuing. "She feels good about moving here. Who would've thought a Philadelphia socialite would ever want to make her home in Fire Mountain?"

Nesto watched Paige's animated face, loving the excitement in her voice. "Yeah. Who knew?"

"It's a great house. You're going to love it." Grabbing her drink, she took a sip, glancing at his plate. "Aren't you hungry?" Setting her cup down, she tilted her head, gaze narrowing when he didn't answer. "Nesto?"

He shook his head, picked up his sandwich, and took a bite. Swallowing, he grabbed his drink. "Let's get out of here when this stuff with Javé is over."

"Out of here?"

"A few days, a week, just the two of us. I don't care where we go—San Diego, the mountains, Santa Fe. You pick the place. We need some time alone without the hassle of work."

Her body relaxed. For an instant, her heart had seized, thinking he'd say something else. "If Brooke will give me the time off. I've only been here a couple weeks."

Reaching across the table, he covered her hand with his. "I'm pretty sure that won't be a problem."

Once they finished eating, he stood. "Ready?"

"I am."

Walking outside, they both froze at the sound of motorcycles, then hurried to Nesto's truck as a group of six bikes pulled into the parking lot. Devil's Sons patches were clearly visible on their jackets.

"We need to get out of here." Nesto settled her in the passenger seat, mumbling a curse when the bikes parked behind the truck, blocking his exit. "No matter what happens, stay inside." Slamming the door, he reached behind him, feeling his Sig Sauer in the small of his back. Walking around the truck, he stepped up to Javé still astride his bike.

"Salgado. Are you having a good day with your woman?"

Crossing his arms, Nesto fixed him with a hard stare. "What do you want? If it's intimidation, you've picked the wrong person."

Chuckling, Javé shook his head. "I have heard that about you, U.S. Marshal Salgado."

"Then you must've already heard I retired months ago. Now, I'll ask again. Why are you blocking my truck?"

"Am I?"

Pulling out his phone, Nesto punched in the number for the police, then held it out so Javé could read the screen. "Your choice."

A hearty laugh burst from Javé's throat. "A misunderstanding, *ex*-Marshal Salgado." Raising his chin, signaling his men, he straightened his bike. Giving a mock salute, he revved the Harley's engine. "Have a good day."

Chapter Eighteen

"Are you sure you're all right, Paige?" Nesto walked beside her, his hand on the small of her back. Even though she'd sworn she was fine, he'd seen how hard she worked to control the shakes on the drive back to the office.

"Yeah."

"I can take you to the ranch house. There's plenty of security there."

Stopping, she turned to look at him, placing a hand on his arm. "I know you're worried about me, but honestly, I'm fine. I was more worried about you." She shook her head, glancing away for a moment before retuning her gaze to his. "If anything happened to you, I..." Her voice trailed off.

Cupping her elbow, he led Paige around the corner of the building, wrapping his arms around her. Tightening his hold, he leaned down next to her ear. "Nothing is going to happen to me, sweetheart. You've got to trust me on that."

Wrapping her arms around his neck, she placed kisses along his jaw and chin, then looked up at him. "I do trust you, Nesto. It's Javé and his men I don't trust."

Taking a deep breath, he rested his chin on the top of her head. "I know what kind of men we're dealing with, babe. So does everyone else. The Sons thrive on intimidation and threats, enjoying the way they can make people squirm. I'm telling you, sweetheart, no one is squirming this time."

A grin spread across her face. "You *were* pretty cool out there."

He returned her smile. "Yeah?"

"If I hadn't been so worried, it might have turned me on."

"Is that right?" He took her mouth, holding her close. Her soft moan had him deepening the kiss, his hands gripping her hips, aligning her body with his. Another moan, louder this time, broke through his lust-filled brain. "Damn, Paige."

She covered her mouth to stop a giggle.

Laughing, Nesto turned her around, swatting her butt. "Get inside before we do something that'll embarrass the hell out of both of us."

Clive and J.D. stared at the computer screen, waiting for Dennis Johnson to start another round of questions. They'd been on the video conference call for over an hour, going over every detail several times. At least the Senior Agent in Charge hadn't said no. They watched the screen, seeing him rub his brows as he scanned the documents again, making notes.

"You realize if I go ahead with this on a formal basis, the two of you will be the lead agents?"

Clive looked at J.D., answering for both of them. "We want to be involved either way, sir."

"How do you propose feeding Robbie the information about Javé's threats without exposing our agent inside Satan's Brethren?"

"Can you get word to him, give the agent a heads-up about what's happening?" Clive asked.

Johnson thought a moment, not looking at the screen, then nodded. "It'll take about twenty-four hours to make it happen."

J.D. leaned forward. "Once he knows, Kade will get in touch with Robbie and request a meeting."

Johnson snorted, shaking his head. "Kade always did have balls of steel. That's one reason it was such a big loss when he left the agency. There's a real possibility he won't walk away from that meeting alive."

J.D. glanced at Clive, then spoke. "He knows this, sir. Ernesto Salgado has volunteered to go with him."

"He's the retired U.S. Marshal and was a U.S. Special Forces operative with Kade, correct?"

Clive nodded. "Yes, sir."

"If anything happens during that meeting, either or both men don't return, we can't have this blow back on the agency." Johnson stared at the screen, his gaze resolute. "It's important those men understand we'll disavow all knowledge of their meeting."

"There is no misunderstanding on that, sir." J.D. checked his notes, looking up. "This has to happen before Friday, the deadline Javé gave Jace MacLaren and Salgado."

Leaning back in his chair, Dennis Johnson steepled his fingers under his chin, then nodded. "Let me get on this. I'll be in touch."

The two agents let out a collective breath as Johnson's image disappeared.

Standing, Clive looked at J.D. "We need to let the boys know."

Picking up their folders, they walked into the hall, seeing Nesto and Kade standing a few feet away.

"Well?" Nesto asked.

A slow smile tipped up the corners of J.D.'s mouth. "We're a go."

Nesto blew out a relieved breath, smiling, as Kade slapped both agents on their backs.

Clive held up a hand. "But we're on hold until Johnson gets word to the agent he has inside Satan's Brethren."

"How long?" Kade asked. "It could take a couple days to set up a meeting with Robbie."

"If he agrees to meet us at all," Nesto added.

"Oh, he'll agree. Whether to exact some twisted sort of revenge on me or to hear what we know involving Amber, he'll meet."

Paige sat next to Sean, studying the last of the data on Serenity Resorts, trying to make sense of the financials.

Dragging a hand through his hair, Sean crossed his arms. "I'm not an accountant, but it seems to me they should have a better bottom line with the amount they charge for their services. Look at what a couple pays for one week at the Idaho location." He pointed to a line on the summary of services the president of Serenity had provided. "Then look at the expenses. They seem way out of line." He glanced at Paige. "I think there's room for lowering expenses in Idaho and Wyoming."

"What about the one in Colorado?"

"I'm not enthusiastic about that one. The operation is small, hasn't done well for a while. Local and state taxes, plus some anti-business regulations, would make it more difficult to recoup our investment anytime soon."

Paige nodded, moving down the list to the hotels. "What are your thoughts on the two Serenity hotels?"

"I know Pops and my uncles want to move in that direction. The problem is this would be our first time in hotel operations. We'd need someone to guide us through it, maybe become the general manager."

Paige used a yellow highlighter to emphasize two names. "Why not keep the managers they already have at each location?"

"It's possible, but the customer reviews I've read aren't good. The properties are upscale with historic designations. The problem seems to be the staff. I'm planning to visit each location next week. I've already been to the dude ranches in Wyoming and Idaho. They're solid. The hotels, not so much." Seeing Nesto standing outside the office, Sean grinned, resting his arm on the back of Paige's chair. "How about you come with me? We could have a great time."

Nesto walked in, sending a warning glare at Sean. "I don't think so."

Raising his hands in surrender, Sean laughed. "I'm just messing with you. I heard the news you two are working things out. Congratulations."

"What if I need to go with Sean?" Paige kept her face neutral.

Nesto rested his hands on his hips. "Then I'd say the locations probably need a security check at the same time."

"We'll make it a threesome," Sean joked, receiving another glare from Nesto. "Probably another bad idea."

Nesto nodded. "One of your worst."

Paige grasped his hand. "How did it go with Dennis Johnson?"

"We're waiting for a decision. From what Clive and J.D. told us, it's going to work out." He leaned down to kiss her.

Sean stood up. "Time for me to pack up my stuff and head out. You two up for drinks?"

Nesto looked at Paige, who shrugged. "Sounds good to me. Having drinks with two handsome men is a great way to end the day."

Walking out of the office, Nesto leaned over, whispering in her ear. "Trust me, babe. Our day won't end with drinks."

"Reyna told me your mom is buying a house in Fire Mountain. Sounds like a great deal for you, Paige." Sean sipped his beer, then grabbed a chip, popping it into his mouth.

Paige nodded, setting her glass of wine down. "She put in an offer today. Three bedroom house near downtown with a great view. Her realtor, a friend of Annie's, thinks it'll be accepted."

"It's a big move. Is your father coming out soon?"

Nesto looked at her, shrugging. Paige picked up her glass, drinking the rest of it before answering.

"My mother is divorcing him. She found out he's had a mistress hidden away for a while."

Sean exhaled a slow breath. "Geez, Paige. I'm sorry. I know what it's like to have your parents split up. In my case, it was my mother who had the affair."

Swallowing the knot threatening to choke her, she clasped her hands in her lap. "He seems happy with Reyna."

Sean nodded. "Pops and Reyna should've married long ago when she was pregnant with Kade. Of course, then I wouldn't be here to torment everyone."

"Or to run the dude ranches," Paige teased.

"You've got me there."

Hearing her phone, she pulled it from her purse, her eyes widening. "It's Paul."

"Answer it. Put it on speaker," Nesto said.

"Paul, where have you been?"

"Paige?"

Her voice trembled with worry. "I'm here. You sound awful. What's going on?"

"Javé and his boys found me." He choked the last out, then sucked in a breath. "I need your help."

Her eyes widened in panic. "I'll call 9-1-1. Where are you?"

"No ambulance. I'm in an alley behind a bank, near downtown. It's bad, Paige."

"Give me the name of the bank." She grabbed paper and a pen out of her purse.

Coughing a couple times, Paul cleared his throat. "First something."

"First Bank," Nesto said.

"We're on our way, Paul." She jumped up, slipping the phone into her purse.

Nesto stood, grabbing Paige's hand.

"I'm riding along." Sean finished his beer and followed them outside.

"He needs a hospital, Paige." Nesto knelt next to him. "I think he has a couple broken ribs, probably a concussion."

Paul grabbed his arm. "No hospital. They'll call the police."

Paige glanced at Nesto, who shook his head.

"Sorry, bro. You're going to the hospital and we'll deal with the consequences." Nesto lifted Paul into his arms, carrying him to the truck.

Sean climbed into the back seat. "Hand him to me." He scooted to one side, taking Paul from Nesto's arms.

Running around the truck, Nesto jumped inside, looking at Paige. "You ready?"

When she nodded, he took off, driving the six blocks to the hospital and straight to the emergency room entrance. A few minutes later, Paul disappeared behind double doors, leaving Paige, Nesto, and Sean to stare after him.

Irene ran up to the desk in the waiting room, her frantic eyes searching for Paige. "Paul Wallace. Where is he?"

"Mother?"

Turning, Irene ran into her daughter's arms.

"The doctor is checking him out now. Nesto thinks he has a couple broken ribs, probably a concussion."

Shaking her head, her mother pulled back, pressing a hand to her forehead. "I don't understand. Why is he in Fire Mountain, and why would someone want to beat him up?"

Paige's lips pressed together, suddenly having second thoughts about calling their mother. "Let's sit down. We should hear something about him soon."

Nesto came up beside them, putting a hand on Irene's back, guiding her to a chair between him and Paige. "From what I saw, there's nothing life threatening. Other than his ribs, I don't think anything else was broken."

Looking at Nesto, her face lined with worry, she clutched his arm. "What happened?"

"We aren't sure. Paul wasn't in good enough condition to tell us. It's a miracle whoever did this didn't take his phone."

Turning, she looked at Paige. "Did you know he was in town?"

"Relatives of Paul Wallace?"

They all stood, walking toward the doctor, Irene in front. "I'm his mother. This is his sister and her fiancé." She looked at Nesto, daring him to deny it.

"Your son is in much better condition than he looks. He has two broken ribs, a couple broken fingers, and numerous lacerations. With care, they'll heal in time." She glanced down at her notes. "The worst injury is a grade two concussion. I'd like to keep him overnight to monitor his recovery."

"Will he be able to go home tomorrow?" Irene asked.

"We'll know more in the morning. If you'd like, I can let two of you in to see him, but only for a few minutes."

Nesto placed a hand on Paige's shoulder. "You and Irene go."

"All right." She kissed his cheek, then turned toward Irene. "Come on, Mother."

Nesto watched as they walked through the doors before pulling out his phone. "Kade. We have trouble."

It took half an hour for Kade, Clive, and J.D. to reach the hospital. By then, Nesto and Sean had discussed what they'd seen and heard, making notes on a pad the woman at the front desk had given them. So far, no police had arrived, for which they were grateful.

"Nesto." Kade hurried to them, pulling up a chair. "What happened?"

They relayed what they knew, pausing to answer questions.

Nesto ran a hand through his hair. "I don't know what Paul did to piss off Javé."

Kade cast a quick look toward the emergency room, shaking his head. "My guess is Paul was a convenient way to send another message to the MacLarens. He's expendable to the club, which isn't good. It would be best for him to heal, then get as far away from here as possible."

Nesto looked at Clive. "What do you think?"

"I think Kade's right. Is he able to answer questions?"

"Paige and Irene are in with him now. The doctor let them go in for five minutes before I called you. A little bit ago, she came back out to say Paul wanted to see them again. I doubt they'll be much longer."

"If no one objects, I'd like for J.D. and I to talk to him for a few minutes. If he'll give us some details, it may provide Johnson a little more incentive to go forward with the plan."

"Works for me," Nesto said, turning to Kade. "Where's Brooke?"

"She's at the main house with her mom and Heath. I told them what happened. Pops took Reyna out for dinner. I called and gave him a heads-up about Paul. I also spoke to Jace. He took it the worst. Wants to go after Javé."

Nesto leaned back in his chair, rubbing his chin. "I'm not surprised. Javé made it a point to tell Jace what he knew of Blake and Brett. It's one thing to see the names of your family listed on a piece of paper. It's another to have the outlaw threatening them to your face. Jace had me hire a bodyguard for each of them."

Sean spoke for the first time since Clive and J.D. arrived. "Blake called me this morning. He's all kinds of ticked off at his dad. Says the bodyguard is already a real pain."

"If you talk to Blake again, tell him to man up," Kade said. "This is important stuff and he'd better get straight with it."

The sound of his phone had Clive stepping a few feet away. His voice carried in the small waiting area, although they couldn't make out what he said. A few minutes later, he walked back, a grim smile on his face.

"That was Johnson. I informed him what's going on here. He told me the agent inside Satan's Brethren knows what's going down. We're ready to move."

Chapter Nineteen

Nesto finished his coffee, watching the sun come up from his front window as Paige rinsed the breakfast dishes. He'd been silent on the plans for him and Kade to meet with Satan's Brethren. She had enough to worry about with her brother in the hospital and Javé's threats. Still, he felt a pang of guilt keeping it from her.

"I'll drive you and Irene to the hospital, then come back to meet with the others."

"I can take Mother to see Paul."

Turning away from the window, his gaze hardened. "No."

"But—"

"This isn't open for discussion, Paige." Walking toward her, he set his empty cup on the counter. "Javé crossed a line when he ordered Paul beaten. Everyone on this ranch is still in danger. Until it's settled, you'll have someone with you wherever you go."

Crossing her arms, Paige leaned a hip against the counter. "I know you're worried about me, Nesto, but I doubt Javé will come after me."

Moving to stand in front of her, he rested his hands on her shoulders, leaning down for a kiss. "I hope you're right, sweetheart." He kissed her again. "You're still not going anywhere alone."

"You're too stubborn for your own good." She pushed past him to grab her purse and laptop.

"Probably."

He had no intention of easing up on security. After last night and Paul swearing to Clive and J.D. it was Javé's men, Nesto had already requested the number of security personnel at the ranch be increased by half.

"I'm ready. Let's go pick up Mother."

"Robbie wants to meet today." Kade pocketed his phone, glancing at the others in his office at MacLaren Enterprises.

"Today? I thought he was at the chapter in Sacramento." Nesto leaned against the wall, his arms crossed.

"Seems he got information late last night about Devil's Sons getting into some shit he didn't know about. They left right afterward. I caught him when they stopped for breakfast."

"We need to know where and when, Kade." Clive stood up, taking the few steps to the window to look outside. "This is short notice for us to set up."

"I've got to go with what he gives me. Robbie will call later with the time and location." He focused his attention on Clive, then looked at J.D. "Do either of you know the undercover agent?"

J.D. shook his head. "Johnson's keeping it close, the same as he did when you went into the Brethren. Why?"

Kade rubbed the back of his neck. "Something seems off. I didn't think the DEA would be able to get anyone else into the Brethren for several years after my true identity became known. It takes time to get inside, be patched in."

"Kade?"

He punched the button on his desk phone to the receptionist. "Yeah."

"There's a man here to see you. Says his name is Thad Montgomery."

Even under the circumstances, a smile spread across Kade's face. "Send him up."

"Timing's everything," J.D. grinned. Both he and Clive knew the former DEA agent who now ran a security and investigative firm for companies doing business in Mexico.

Stepping into the hall, Kade moved to intercept Thad as he came up the steps. Holding out his hand, he pulled him into a quick embrace. "Hey, man. It's good to see you."

"Same here. I heard you might need some help. Something about a tussle with the Sons."

Kade pinched the bridge of his nose. "Where'd you hear that?" he asked before his features stilled. "Gage Templeton."

"The one and only. He caught me just as I finished unloading the last box at my new home in the Hill Country outside Austin. Thought I'd fly out, see if I can help."

Clasping him on the back, Kade turned him toward his office. "You came at the right time." Opening the door, Thad stopped.

"Looks like you've got a whole team already." He walked in, shaking hands with J.D., Clive, and Nesto.

"Are you ready to be briefed in?" Nesto asked.

"Give me a cup of coffee and I'm all yours."

Sometime early morning, the doctor cleared Paul to move into the private room Heath MacLaren arranged. He hurt all over, including a monstrous headache, made worse when the nurse opened the blinds.

"Geez..." He placed an arm over his eyes to shut out the glare.

"Sorry, Mr. Wallace." Closing them, she began the routine of checking his vitals, finishing as Paige and Irene walked in. They nodded at Paul, saying nothing until the nurse left.

"Have you seen the doctor this morning?" Irene asked, pulling a chair next to the bed.

"Not yet." He glanced away, not able to accept the worried expression on his mother's face.

"How do you feel?" Paige set another chair next to Irene.

He looked at Paige, licking his dry lips. "Like someone dropped me off a two hundred foot cliff."

Paige leaned forward, touching his arm. "The doctor said you were lucky. She told us the worst is the concussion."

"She told me the same. Look, I need to get out of here. I can't stand them poking and prodding me any longer."

Irene shook her head. "Not until the doctor releases you. Then we'll take you back to the ranch. You can stay in the guest room at Nesto's cabin."

"No, Mother. I'm leaving the country. Heading up to Canada."

Irene's eyes widened. "Canada? Why would you do that?"

"Javé wants me dead. I can't stay around here any longer." His gaze shifted to Paige for a brief moment before he closed his eyes. "Sorry, Paige. I know I've put you in danger."

Her mouth drew into a thin line. "You aren't going anywhere, Paul. You're going to stay here and testify against Javé."

Opening his eyes, a look of hope passed over his face. "They arrested him?"

"No, but it's just a matter of time. He isn't going to get away with blackmailing the MacLarens."

Paul tried to sit up, then fell back against the pillow. "You don't know Javé. They'll never get enough to put him in jail."

Paige thought of the look on Nesto's face this morning. The same determination and confidence she'd seen when he was about to confront a difficult assignment. Even if he hadn't shared any information with her, she knew he and Kade had a plan. She also believed, with all her heart, they'd be able to find a way out of this mess and put Javé behind bars.

"You need to have a little faith in Nesto and Kade. They've been in worse situations and made it out."

"Get a grip, Paige. This isn't some mission in special ops where they have well-trained men and a truckload of fire power. Outlaw gangs don't work within any rules. Worse, they have police, sheriffs, and even DEA agents on their payroll."

Irene shook her head. "Paul, that can't be true."

"It definitely is true, Mother."

"How do you know?" Paige asked.

"I've been with Javé and his men when they've been drunk, lost their inhibitions. No specifics, but they all bragged about who actually owned law enforcement in their territory. It's bad, Paige. I doubt even the DEA agents who spoke to me last night know about it."

"What don't Clive and J.D. know, Paul? You have to tell us."

He started to shake his head, moaning as intense pain assaulted him.

"What's going on?" The doctor walked into the room, seeing Paul's face twist in agony. "Mr. Wallace, you need to rest." Checking the monitors, she looked at Paige and Irene. "Why don't you step into the hall for a minute while he settles down."

Nodding, the women started to move, stopping when Paul called out. "Wait. You need to tell Nesto."

Paige stepped next to the bed. "What do I need to tell Nesto?"

Closing his eyes, Paul inhaled a deep breath before looking at his sister. "There's a DEA agent on Javé's payroll. Part-Hispanic guy. I don't know his name." He closed his eyes again.

"He needs to rest a while."

Paige's heart pounded. "I know, Doctor, but he needs to finish."

"I'm sorry, but now isn't—"

"Satan's Brethren." Paul's eyes opened to slits.

They looked at Paul, Paige touching his arm. "What about Satan's Brethren?"

He let out a breath, looking at her. "Javé's man. He's inside Satan's Brethren."

Nesto looked at his phone, seeing Paige's name. He slid it back into his pocket without answering. Kade stood at his desk, his phone to his ear as he jotted down the location and time of the meeting with Robbie. Whatever Paige needed would have to wait.

Ending the call, Kade looked at the men in the room. "Six o'clock at Valley Repair."

Nesto nodded. "I've been there with Mitch. He had them check something out on his bike."

Clive opened a map application on his phone, noting the location. "Robbie will have backup with him."

Kade dragged a hand through his hair. "He'll bring his VP and sergeant-at-arms. The others will wait outside with the bikes."

Nesto stepped next to him. "I'll be with you, bro. So will Thad." He could imagine what was going through his friend's mind. The same as what was going through his after all this time away. He knew Kade wanted to put that part of his life behind him. It wasn't to be.

"We've got two hours to set this up. Let's get started." Clive pulled up a satellite image of Valley Repair on Kade's computer. "Nesto, tell us about the layout."

He walked up to the computer, pointing at each section. "Office on the right. Service bays on the left. Storage room and bathroom here and here. I noticed one exit to the back parking area. There may be one out of the office, as well."

J.D. rested his hands on the desk, leaning forward to get a better view of the image. "Thorough, Nesto."

"Yeah. I like to know where I'm having my bike fixed."

Kade chuckled. "What Nesto means is he's blatantly suspicious about new surroundings."

"Lucky for us." Clive changed the view to the front. "At six in the evening, I'd suspect the place to be closed. I've got to guess Satan's Brethren has a connection to the place. Kade, Nesto, and Thad go inside at the same time as Robbie and his crew, and you go in armed. J.D. and I will park near the bikes, schmooze with the men Robbie leaves outside."

J.D. stepped away, crossing his arms. "Anything else before we take off?"

"Any chance local law knows anything about what's going down?" Nesto asked.

"If you're asking if Johnson has given the sheriff a heads-up, not to my knowledge." Clive looked at J.D.

"Something like this, it's doubtful he'd bring others into it. Johnson wants this to fly under the radar. Can't do that if you have local law involved." J.D. shook his head. "I'd say no."

Nesto felt his phone vibrate in his pocket and checked the screen. Paige again.

"Is it an emergency?" Kade stood next to him. "We need to go."

He shook his head, sliding the phone back into his pocket. "No. Let's go."

Paige paced back and forth in the waiting area closest to Paul's room. She knew what he told her about Javé's man being inside Satan's Brethren was important. Nesto needed to know, but her calls had gone to voicemail twice. After the second attempt, she'd called the office, learning he'd left with Kade, J.D., and Clive. Paige hoped he'd get the messages.

Sean walked into the waiting area, followed by Matt and Mitch. "How is he?" Sean asked, coming up to Paige.

She shook her head, seeing Matt take a seat next to her mother. "Truthfully, I don't know. The wounds to his body will heal. I'm not sure about what's going on inside his head."

"Did he confirm it was Javé's men?" Mitch asked.

"Yes. He told Clive and J.D. the same last night." She caught her lower lip between her teeth.

Sean placed a hand on her shoulder. "What is it?"

"Paul told me something I think Nesto and Kade need to know. I've called Nesto, but he didn't answer, and I don't know if he's listened to my messages."

"Tell us," Mitch said.

"Paul told me Javé has people inside law enforcement. The police, sheriff, and..." She swallowed, still not quite believing it.

"What?" Sean asked.

"Javé has a DEA agent on his payroll. The man is a member of Satan's Brethren."

Mitch mumbled a curse, grabbing his phone, hurrying outside. Looking around to be sure no one could hear him, he tapped Nesto's number. When it went to voicemail, he called Kade. He left a message for each one. *Call me right away. It's important.* He tried one more number.

"Pops, it's Mitch."

"What do you need, son?"

"Do you have any idea where Nesto and Kade are?"

Rafe exhaled. They'd made a conscious decision to keep what was going on within a small group of people—the five men who left to meet Robbie, plus Heath, Jace, and him.

"Why do you ask?"

"I'll take that as a yes. Look, I don't know what's going on, but Paul Wallace told Paige something she believes is important. Nesto and Kade aren't answering their phones. I'm hoping you can get a message to them."

"Go ahead." Rafe listened, taking notes until he dropped the pen on the desk. "I've got it, Mitch. Let me see if I can reach one of them." Hanging up, he dialed Kade, praying his son answered.

"There it is." Nesto nodded to the building a few yards ahead. "I don't see any bikes."

"I'm guessing they're waiting for us to show up, then they'll ride in, showing unity and a wall of force." Kade leaned forward in the seat, sliding his Sig into the waistband of his pants at the small of his back. He glanced over his shoulder. "You ready, Thad?"

Thad slid his Sig into its holster. "I am now."

"Go on in, Nesto. Park so the front of the truck is pointed toward the road. Stay inside until the Brethren get here."

Nesto nodded, parking as Kade directed, leaving the engine running.

Thad looked around from the back seat. "Here they come."

Within seconds, the deep rumble of motorcycles filled the air before a dozen bikes circled the truck and stopped. Kade recognized Robbie right away.

"Party's on, boys." Kade opened the door, climbing out. Nesto and Thad did the same. His gaze took in each of the riders, recognizing some. The VP and sergeant-at-arms were the same as when he was embedded in the club. Neither acknowledged him.

Moving forward, Kade halted as Robbie got off his bike. The next few seconds passed in the blink of an eye. Robbie stepped forward, pulled back his right arm, and nailed Kade in the jaw.

Nesto and Thad started to move.

"Not smart, boys." The club VP held a gun pointed at Nesto. "Prez has some business to finish before we go inside and talk."

As the words came out, Robbie kicked Kade twice in the chest, then once in the thigh, stopping when another truck pulled into the lot, stopping within feet of Robbie.

Climbing out of the truck, Clive walked up to Robbie, glancing down at Kade.

"You don't want to hear what our friend has to say, no skin off our teeth. We'll take our boy and go." Kneeling, Clive started to lift Kade.

"Leave him," Robbie said through gritted teeth.

"No can do. He came here to warn you about a betrayal in your ranks. Oh yeah, and the fact your daughter has been targeted by one of your associated clubs. Frankly, I don't give a damn about either." Clive helped Kade stand, checking the injuries. "We'll be seeing you boys." Putting an arm around Kade's waist, they started for the truck.

"What about Amber?"

Kade coughed, wincing in pain. "Stop, Clive. I'm good."

He lowered his voice. "I know you are, man. This was all for show." Clive stepped away, nodding to Nesto and Thad before returning to stand next to J.D.

Kade coughed again, holding an arm tight to his chest as he turned around. "Damn, Robbie. I think you broke some ribs."

Robbie looked him over, snorting. "You'll survive. He said you have information about Amber."

"I do. Plus some other stuff I think you'll find interesting."

Robbie nodded. "Let's go inside. I'm warning you, Kade. This better be worth it."

Kade signaled Nesto and Thad, who followed them inside, along with Robbie's two officers. Closing the door, Robbie turned toward Kade.

"Talk."

It took several minutes for Kade to explain Javé's threats to the MacLarens, the information the Sons' president had about Amber, the intimidation, and the beating of Paul. Robbie didn't interrupt, his features devoid of emotion. The only sign the threat to Amber bothered him was the way his hands fisted at his sides, tapping his thighs as Kade finished.

Nostrils flaring, Robbie took a step toward him. "What else? I know there's more."

Kade opened his mouth, closing it at a pounding on the door.

Robbie motioned for Nesto to open it, spotting Clive standing there with his phone in his hand.

"I've got news. It's important." He held it out, letting Nesto read the text message from Rafe. "You've got to get this to Kade."

Taking the phone from Clive's hand, Nesto closed the door, walking up to Kade, not taking his eyes off Robbie. "He's got to see this. It has to do with the Brethren." Robbie gave a tight nod.

Grabbing the phone, Kade read through it, his face neutral. Handing it back to Nesto, he approached Robbie.

"We have to talk in private." Kade glanced behind him, locking gazes with the VP. "Just you and me."

Robbie stared at him for a moment, then looked at his two men. "Wait outside with the others."

Kade nodded at Nesto and Thad, silently telling them to do the same. The instant the door closed behind them, Robbie walked to a bench and sat down.

"Take a load off and tell me the rest."

Thirty minutes later, after bouts of yelling, cursing, and pacing, the two settled down to carve out a plan.

"You're a bastard, Kade. Using Amber to help me solve the MacLaren's mess."

"Never said I wasn't."

"I don't trust you."

"Didn't think you would, Robbie. Right now, trusting me isn't high on my list of priorities."

Scrubbing a hand down his face, Robbie paced some more, then looked at Kade. "That sonofabitch."

"You know who the mole is, don't you?"

Kade couldn't let Robbie kill the man who'd been undercover since before Kade was patched in to Satan's Brethren. The man might be working both sides, but he deserved his say in front of Dennis Johnson. He'd earned that right.

"Yeah, I know. It's club business. I'll handle it."

"Can't let you do that, Robbie."

"Unless you've got a damn good alternative in mind, I'll take care of this my own way."

Kade stood, wincing as he leaned against a workbench, crossing his arms. "You're facing years in prison on various charges."

Robbie barked out a laugh, holding his arms out. "Do you see me sitting in a jail cell?"

"Here's the deal." Kade proceeded to list a few choice bits of information the DEA already had, how it was weeks, maybe days before a major raid on the club. By the look in Robbie's eyes, he could see the outlaw already knew all of it. The club had been under intense scrutiny for months, knowing it would all crash down on them soon.

"You go after Javé. Do whatever you have to do to a club who's going behind your back, threatening your daughter, and establishing distribution outside the agreement you two carved out. Hell, destroy them for all I care. They're no use to you now anyway. But I want the mole."

"What do I get for all this Good Samaritan bull?"

"Reduced sentences to lesser charges. Help for your old ladies and kids while you're in jail. A case of whiskey waiting for you the day you get out."

"Hell, Kade. You always did know what was most important to me." Shredding a hand through his hair, Robbie walked a few feet away, then spun back around, pointing a finger at Kade. "You get me all this in writing. When I see it, we'll take care of your mess."

“And the mole.”

“I’ll keep him alive for you. Beyond that, no promises.”

Kade walked up to him, getting within a couple inches of Robbie’s face. “You sure as hell *will* promise if you want to see a reduction in charges and time. Getting the man out of here is *not* negotiable.”

For a few strained moments, Robbie glared at Kade, his jaw hardening. Finally, he stuck out his hand. “You’d better not cross me on this. If you do, there will be no place you can hide.”

Chapter Twenty

"You promised *what*?" Dennis Johnson's voice roared over the video conference call the following morning. Even hundreds of miles away, Kade leaned back in his chair.

"It's all spelled out in the—"

"I know where it's spelled out, Taylor. I've got it right in front of me." Johnson flashed the paper in front of the screen.

"It's MacLaren, sir."

"I don't give a damn what your last name is now, you are way out of line. And you aren't even with the agency any longer." Looking at his desk, Johnson mumbled, just loud enough for those in the conference room to hear. "For the love of all that's holy, how do I get myself into such messes?"

"Sir?"

Johnson looked at the screen. "You got anything good to say, Agent Nelson?"

Clive got straight to the point. "Your man is compromised. Robbie knows who he is, and unless we agree to the terms Kade laid out, the agent will be skinned and buried somewhere in the desert. Then there's the threat to the MacLarens and Javé's connection to the cartels."

"Possible connection, Agent Nelson. I've seen no hard proof."

"It's there, sir. Given enough time, we'll find it."

"And you, Agent Montalban. What is your take on this?"

"For what we'll get from Robbie, it's a good deal. He'll crush Devil's Sons, protect the MacLarens, and turn over your agent. My guess is he thinks he and his brothers are facing twenty or more years behind bars. Reduced charges would still get him ten to fifteen. They'll be old and obsolete by the time they get out."

"A younger group will take over," Johnson replied.

J.D. held firm. "That's always the case, sir."

Johnson rubbed his chin, shaking his head. "I hesitate to ask, but I want your thoughts on this, ex-Agent Montgomery."

"It's good to see you again, sir."

"Don't try your bull on me, Thad."

"Yes, sir." He cleared his throat. "I agree with the others. If there's a way to pull this off, it'd be a helluva deal. I'll bet you'd get a commendation—"

"Save it, Montgomery. Salgado, I'm guessing you feel the same."

"I do, sir, except for one detail." Nesto could feel Kade's gaze boring into him.

"Spit it out, Salgado."

"I'd like to see Javé taken alive. There's a good chance of getting him to talk, give up his contacts in the cartel."

"What more could we offer Robbie to keep Javé alive? He's going to want to cut the man's head off."

"Take one charge off the table." Nesto held up his hand when Kade tried to interrupt.

Johnson pinched the bridge of his nose. "What would that be?"

"Prostitution. It's worth next to nothing against the other charges, but it may sweeten the deal enough with Robbie that he'll hand Javé over alive."

The men watched Johnson's image on the screen as he scribbled a few notes, then looked up.

"You all know if I agree to this, it could end my career."

"Yes, sir," Kade said as the others nodded.

Johnson tossed down his pen, leaning back in his chair. "It'll be a helluva way to go out. All right, go with the plan with Salgado's one change. I'll have it in writing in a few minutes. And, gentlemen, I want Agent Joshua Beltran alive. That's it. Keep me posted."

The screen went blank to stunned silence. No one moved for several moments as each man accepted the final verdict.

"He's with us," Nesto mumbled.

"Hell yeah, he is." Clive clasped him on the shoulder.

A few minutes later, Kade's computer signaled the arrival of an email. A smile spread across his face when he opened the document, letting everyone read it.

Clive whistled. "It's a done deal, gentlemen. Kade, do you want to call Robbie?"

"I'm on it." Moving to the other end of the room, he tapped Robbie's number. "It's Kade. Got the okay. Meet in an hour, the same place as last night. You get the deal in writing, I leave with the mole."

Paige couldn't sit still, finding it impossible to concentrate on what Sean was saying about Serenity Resorts. Nesto had called late the night before, apologizing for not taking her calls, assuring her everything was all right.

They'd talked for twenty minutes before Nesto told her he wouldn't be home. He and the other men were locking themselves in the office to finalize an agreement that could keep Javé away from them permanently.

Mitch had driven her and Brooke to the ranch house after work. Nesto told her they'd be spending the night with Annie and Heath. Paige didn't like it, but he'd given her no choice.

"Hey."

She spun toward the door at the sound of Nesto's voice. Rushing to him, she wrapped her arms around his neck, holding tight.

"I think she's glad to see you." Sean left the room, giving them a few minutes alone.

"I was so worried." She kissed his neck, his jaw, his lips, assuring herself he was all right.

"I know, babe," he breathed against her mouth. "We don't have much time. We're leaving in a few minutes for a meeting. If all goes well, we'll be able to put the events of the past few weeks behind us."

The lines of worry on her face relaxed a little. "You're sure?"

"As certain as I can be until we've had the meeting." Stepping away, he looked at the paperwork on the desk. "Any progress with Serenity?"

"How can you talk about Serenity at a time like this?"

He chuckled as he leaned against the table, slipping his arm around her waist, drawing her to him. "How's Paul?"

"Doing better. Says he's leaving for Canada as soon as the doctor releases him."

Nesto's brows lifted. "He's still in the hospital?"

"He keeps slipping in and out of consciousness. He'll be released by this weekend."

The door opened again, Clive poking his head inside. "We're ready."

Nodding, Nesto kissed her. "I've got to go. I'll find you as soon as I get back."

"I love you."

He smiled. "Love you, too, Paige."

Kade watched as Robbie read the agreement Johnson sent. Nesto and Thad stood behind the chair where the Brethren's VP, Joshua Beltran, had been secured with zip ties. The club's sergeant-at-arms stood a few feet away, looking as if he'd much prefer gutting the man instead of turning him over. As it was, Beltran had two bruised and swollen eyes, a split lip, and what appeared to be a broken arm. Kade guessed he'd find more injuries under Josh's clothes.

Robbie looked up. "It's all here. I can't guarantee the part about Javé. You know how it is, Kade."

"Yeah, I do. The rest stays, even if you can't give us Javé."

Robbie looked at Josh, eyes narrowed. "If I ever see him again, he's fair game."

"Understood."

Robbie scribbled his signature on the document, handing it to Kade. "Take Beltran and get out of here before I change my mind and slit his throat...and yours. I have a war to plan."

Nesto had borrowed Heath's large SUV, knowing there'd be six of them coming back. What he hadn't expected was Beltran's condition. They folded down the third seat, allowing Thad and J.D. to help him position himself so his back didn't touch anything. With that completed, they jumped into the SUV, heading for town.

Once they got a mile away, J.D. told Nesto to stop. Getting out, he dashed to the back and opened the doors.

"Turn around, Beltran. We need to get that jacket off you."

Josh cursed as the jacket, then his shirt came off, revealing fresh injuries to his back.

"What the hell did they use on you?" Thad asked.

"The cat," Josh answered through gritted teeth.

Clive's brows lifted. "A cat o' nine tails?"

"One of the brothers is from Trinidad. He has several stashed away. I've never known him to use any of them before this morning." Josh winced when J.D. dampened a cloth, trying to clean out the dirt.

Thad looked at Nesto. "We need to get him to the hospital."

"No. You can't take me there."

J.D. capped the bottle of water, setting down the cloth. "You're in bad shape, man. These will get infected if they're not treated. Plus, it looks like your arm is broken."

Shaking his head, Josh adjusted himself so he could ride with as little discomfort as possible. "You all know the drill. Call Johnson. Have him send men to pick me up. They'll know what to do."

"It's your funeral, man." J.D. closed the door, returning to his seat before Nesto rolled out.

Passing a strip mall not far from the ranch, a black SUV pulled out behind them, keeping pace all the way to the entrance of the ranch.

"We're being followed." Kade adjusted his outside mirror, keeping the vehicle in sight. "I think your guys are already here, Beltran."

Grimacing, Josh looked out the back window. "Yeah. That's them."

The car followed them until Nesto stopped about a quarter mile up the ranch driveway. "Looks like this is where you get off, Beltran."

Few words passed between them as they helped Josh out, then turned to face two agents walking toward them. A few feet away, the men showed their badges, introducing themselves, eyes focused on Josh. One pulled out his phone, talking in a low voice as he walked away.

When the other one walked up to support Josh under an arm, Clive stopped him.

"One arm's probably broken, maybe some ribs, too. Where are you taking him?"

He nodded toward the man on the phone. "We're getting that set up now. He'll get treated within the hour." Returning his attention to Josh, he shook his head. "Dammit, Josh. We told you to get the hell out of there months ago. Now look at you."

One corner of Josh's mouth turned up into a grim smile. "As long as the shit on my face heals, I'll be fine."

"Always thinking of the ladies." The agent shook his head. "Come on, man. Let's get you in the car."

Josh held up a hand. "Hold on." Turning, he looked at Kade. "Sorry I couldn't let you in on what was going on. We were into dangerous shit, and you know how Sonny and Robbie are. I was too high up to make any mistakes. No hard feelings." He extended his hand to Kade, who took it.

"No hard feelings."

"So you know, I never worked for Javé. It was all an elaborate ruse Johnson concocted. Maybe one of us will share the story with you sometime."

"Take a leave when they cut you some time. Come stay at the ranch for a while."

Josh nodded. "I just might do that."

After the agents disappeared with Josh, Nesto turned the SUV around, driving to the office. It was noon by the time he parked the car in the lot and they all climbed out, heading inside.

An hour later, they emerged from a meeting with Heath, Rafe, and Jace. All they could do now was wait and hope Robbie didn't renege on the deal.

"I'm going to find Brooke. Meet us for dinner tonight. You pick the place."

"Sure thing."

Nesto didn't let his guard down as he walked down the long hallway toward the meeting room where Paige and Sean worked. He'd seen too many deals crash and burn while working as a U.S. Marshal. He didn't expect anything to happen this time, but he didn't want to tempt fate. Pushing open the door, he relaxed when his gaze settled on Paige. Glancing up, she stood, letting out a deep breath as she walked up to him.

She wound her arms around his neck, looking up. "How did it go?"

He looked at Sean, then back at Paige. "The deal is in place. Now we wait for word on how Robbie is going to handle Devil's Sons. I doubt it will take long. We brought a man back with us. An undercover agent inside Satan's Brethren. He told us Robbie called in two other chapters. My guess is no less than forty Brethren will meet tonight to plan Javé's fate." He wanted to lift her into his arms, take her home and to bed. Instead, he leaned down to kiss her, then stepped away, looking at Sean. "How are you doing with Serenity?"

"I think we may have a good plan for acquiring most of their business. What do you think, Paige?"

"Sean's right. He's the one who came up with the proposal."

Nesto shook his head. "Please don't tell me he's the brains in this room."

"Hey." Sean smiled in protest.

"Actually, yes. We're meeting with the brothers in a couple hours. Here." Paige handed him the draft. "Read through this. Let us know if you see any holes. I'm heading to the ladies' room."

Groaning, Nesto took the papers from her and sat down, his gaze meeting Sean's. "Is it a good deal?"

"Once I found a few, uh…discrepancies in their data, it became a great deal. Pops and my uncles are going to love it."

The rest of the day passed in a blur as Nesto got back up to speed on his regular duties. Admitting he didn't know much about the financial aspects of the deal, he'd seen little to object to in the proposal to purchase Serenity. The brothers agreed, giving Sean the okay to continue. The one remaining acquisition, Champion Horse Breeding, needed Kade's review.

After dinner with Kade and Brooke, Nesto and Paige drove to his cabin, heading straight to bed. It had been too long since they spent time exploring each other, taking their time, reveling in the comfort of each other's body. At midnight, Paige drifted off to sleep, her head tucked under his chin, a hand on his chest. He couldn't remember a time he'd felt so complete.

When the sun came up, he kissed her forehead, then slipped out of bed. Over the course of the last week, their relationship had shifted. He felt it and believed Paige did, as well.

Grabbing his phone, he sent a short text to Heath, getting a swift reply. Grinning, he returned to the bedroom.

"Hey." Paige reached out to him. "Where'd you go?"

Kissing her, he leaned back. "Making plans for today. Let's go for a ride."

She sat up, brushing the hair off her face. "But work..."

"Already cleared it with Heath. We've got the morning off." Holding out his hand, he led her to the shower.

He'd ridden the ranch enough to know exactly where he wanted to end up. While they saddled their horses, Annie had been kind enough to prepare them a snack, giving each a kiss on the cheek before they mounted.

"You picked a perfect day, Nesto."

"Yeah. Wish I could dial it up like this every morning." Reining Ghost next to Daisy, a chestnut mare Paige liked, he held out his hand. For a few minutes, they rode in silence, enjoying the day and the feel of their intertwined fingers.

"Do you have a place in mind?"

Chuckling, he nodded. "I do. If the creek is running, the water comes down in a short waterfall about a mile up ahead."

"Sounds beautiful."

A few minutes later, Nesto reined Ghost to a stop, dismounted, then helped Paige down. "We'll leave the horses here." Reaching into his saddlebags, he removed the food, handing it to Paige, then untied the blanket. "This way." He grabbed her hand, willing his racing heart to slow down as they got closer to the spot he had in mind. Rounding a corner, he heard Paige's intake of breath.

"It's beautiful." She walked to the edge of the creek, peering over a drop-off where the water tumbled into a lagoon twenty feet below. "Have you ever gone swimming in there?"

"Nope. We'll have to do it when we have more time. I'm starving. Let's eat."

Spreading out the blanket, Nesto handed her a sandwich, waiting as she unwrapped it.

"It's been a tough few weeks. I know it wasn't what you expected when you moved from Philadelphia." Twisting off the cap of a water bottle, he held it out to her, then opened one for himself.

"No. It's better."

His brows furrowed, his head tilting to one side. "What do you mean?"

Setting the sandwich and the bottle in her lap, she reached out to cup his face. "You and me. I never dared hope we'd have a second chance. I was so foolish, Nesto."

Placing his hand over hers, he nodded. "A foolish heart, huh?"

"In the worst way."

"I think we can make it better."

Reaching into his pocket, he pulled out the small box he'd packed away two years before. He never thought he'd have a chance to offer it to Paige, but he could never quite let it go. Opening it, he held it out to Paige.

"Marry me. Have my children. Build the life we always dreamed of, Paige."

Her eyes were wide, a hand covering her mouth as tears welled in her eyes. She couldn't speak, the lump in her throat too thick to form words.

His gaze narrowed. "Paige?"

Nodding, she threw herself across the blanket and into his arms. "Yes. Always yes."

They took longer than the four hours Nesto had requested. By the time they reached the office late Friday afternoon, the place had quieted, some employees already gone for the weekend.

Holding her hand, Nesto led her up the stairs to Kade's office. "You sure you want Kade and Brooke to know before your mother and Paul?"

"Absolutely. Without them, we never would've met."

Knocking, Nesto opened the door at the sound of Kade's voice. They were in luck. Brooke sat on his lap, both looking at something on the computer screen.

Brooke looked up. "Where have you two been?"

Paige glanced at Nesto. "We, um…"

Nesto grabbed her left hand, holding it up.

"You're engaged?" Brooke got off Kade's lap, wrapping Paige in a hug.

Standing, Kade slapped Nesto on the back. "Congratulations, bro. It's a good move."

"Thanks. It's definitely time." Glancing over Kade's shoulder, Nesto stared at the image on the screen.

"Have you heard the news?" Kade turned the laptop so they could see the screen. "An explosion leveled an old warehouse about thirty miles from here. More than twenty casualties, and they expect more. So far, all they're saying is a gas leak is suspected of causing the explosion."

Paige leaned forward for a better look as Nesto's gaze locked on Kade.

"A gas leak, huh?" Nesto's face gave nothing away.

Kade nodded, tugging Brooke a little closer. "That's what the reporter is saying. It's so far out in the boonies, no one was close enough to see it. Probably took whoever was inside by complete surprise."

"What a shame."

Again, Kade nodded. "Yeah. A real shame."

Epilogue

Three weeks later...

Nesto held Paige's hand, wishing he could haul her back to the cabin, disappearing behind closed doors for the rest of the day. It wouldn't happen. Gage and Skye had just exchanged their vows, and after all the work Annie, Reyna, and Caroline had put in, no one would be leaving the reception anytime soon.

"It's a shame Gage's parents and brother couldn't be here."

Nesto brushed a strand of hair from her face, kissing her cheek. "According to Skye, there's something going on within the family. Gage hasn't seen his brother in a few years. Doesn't even acknowledge him. I feel bad for the guy."

"It's hard when there are problems within the family." Paige watched her mother circulate through the crowd, a sight she'd witnessed many times growing up. Irene was the consummate hostess, making certain everyone had drinks and food, even hustling others onto the dance floor the men had set up early that morning.

"Irene looks happy." Nesto squeezed her hand, then lifted it to his lips, kissing her wrist.

Paige knew she'd never get tired of her affectionate man. "She does. I think having her own place far away from Philadelphia and Father's antics is what Mother needed."

Nesto looked at her. "Antics? A strange way to talk about his cheating. Has he contacted her since being served the divorce papers?"

"Not a word. From what Mother heard, he hasn't contacted his attorney, either. He did return from his trip to Europe a little early—without the girlfriend."

"How'd you find that out?" Nesto nodded to Kade and Brooke standing a few feet away, talking with Mitch and Dana.

A wry grin spread across Paige's face. "His secretary and I go way back."

"Ah." Nesto rocked on his heels. "Maybe your parents will end up working things out."

Shaking her head, she sighed. "Mother says there's no chance of a reconciliation. He cheated and that's it for her." She looked up at Nesto. "Her words, not mine."

"I'd feel the same in her situation." He smiled at Kade and Brooke as they walked toward them.

Nesto clasped Kade on the shoulder. "Quite a turnout. I thought Gage might change his mind at the last minute and put Skye on a plane for Vegas."

"From what I heard, it was a close decision." Kade grinned as he draped an arm over Brooke's shoulders.

"Did you hear anything more from Clive or J.D. about Josh Beltran?" Nesto kept his gaze moving across the crowd, a habit he didn't intend to break anytime soon. Javé Cruz, a little beaten and bloodied from the explosion at the Devil's Sons' clubhouse, was being held under tight security. Several of the members were on a run at the time, and if the rumor mill was accurate, they had plans to retaliate. Nesto hoped their revenge didn't include the MacLarens.

"Clive called last night. Josh is doing fine. Whatever happened with him in the Brethren, Johnson backed up his story. The guy's got a boatload of data on the entire club. I told Clive to remind Beltran of the offer to vacation in Fire Mountain. He grew up on his parents' ranch in Texas. Might get him out here for our annual cattle drive."

"I'm going," Brooke said, resting a hand on her extended belly.

Kissing her cheek, Kade shook his head. "I don't think so, darlin' Too close to your due date."

"I'll go." Paige looked at Nesto, daring him to say no.

"Sounds good to me, sweetheart."

Paige looked across the crowd. "Who are Sean and Thad talking to?"

Nesto followed her gaze. "The slim one with the long auburn hair is Nicole MacLaren. She's Sean's cousin. The last I knew, she had moved back to her parents' ranch near Austin. I've never seen the other woman. Let's go meet her and I'll introduce you to Nikki."

"We're going over to talk with Pops and Mom. Catch up with you later, bro." Kade tugged on Brooke's hand, laughing when he saw her glaring at him. "Sorry, babe, but no riding until after the baby comes."

"I hear congratulations are in order." Nikki walked up to Nesto, giving him a kiss on the cheek.

"Thanks, Nikki. This is my fiancée, Paige Wallace. Paige, this is Nicole MacLaren."

"Please, call me Nikki." She held out her hand.

Paige grasped it. "It's a pleasure to meet you. I didn't know there were any MacLarens in Texas."

"Quite a number of us, I'm afraid. This is Ellie Russell."

Paige shook her hand. "Nice to meet you."

Nikki looked at her friend. "Ellie has an interview with Heath this week, so she decided to come a couple days early to meet a few people."

Sean lifted a brow. "An interview, huh? I didn't know we had any openings. What do you do?"

Ellie looked at Sean, her bright smile causing his heart to accelerate. "My degree is in hospitality management. I've worked in hotels since high school. It seemed natural to continue with it in college."

Sean stared at her, his jaw tightening, but he didn't interrupt. His body noticed Ellie the moment Nikki introduced them. Long dark hair falling over her shoulders, bright green eyes with a hint of amusement in them. He guessed her to be about five-foot-four. Too short for him, but who cared. Sean's idea had been to convince her a night with him before she flew home would be a great way to spend her time. The idea evaporated in a split second when he learned Ellie's reason for coming to Fire Mountain.

"I'm with a large corporate chain now and hate it. I'm looking for something smaller with more intimate contact with the clientele."

"Intimate?" Sean choked out.

She tilted her head at him. "You know. Get to know the customers so they feel special."

Sean glanced at Kade, who shook his head before looking down at the ground, smirking. "And you're interviewing for what position?"

"General Manager of the new acquisition—Serenity Resorts."

If you enjoyed Foolish Heart, I'd suggest the Macklins of Whiskey Bend Contemporary Western Romance series!

If you want to keep current on all my preorders, new releases, and other happenings, sign up for my newsletter: https://www.shirleendavies.com/contact-me.html

A Note from Shirleen

Thank you for taking the time to read **Foolish Heart**!

If you enjoyed it, please consider telling your friends or posting a short review. Word of mouth is an author's best friend and much appreciated.

I care about quality, so if you find something in error, please contact me via email at shirleen@shirleendavies.com

Books by Shirleen Davies

Contemporary Western Romance Series

MacLarens of Fire Mountain

Second Summer, Book One
Hard Landing, Book Two
One More Day, Book Three
All Your Nights, Book Four
Always Love You, Book Five
Hearts Don't Lie, Book Six
No Getting Over You, Book Seven
'Til the Sun Comes Up, Book Eight
Foolish Heart, Book Nine

Macklins of Whiskey Bend

Thorn, Book One
Del, Book Two
Boone, Book Three

Historical Western Romance Series

Redemption Mountain

Redemption's Edge, Book One
Wildfire Creek, Book Two
Sunrise Ridge, Book Three

Dixie Moon, Book Four
Survivor Pass, Book Five
Promise Trail, Book Six
Deep River, Book Seven
Courage Canyon, Book Eight
Forsaken Falls, Book Nine
Solitude Gorge, Book Ten
Rogue Rapids, Book Eleven
Angel Peak, Book Twelve
Restless Wind, Book Thirteen
Storm Summit, Book Fourteen
Mystery Mesa, Book Fifteen
Thunder Valley, Book Sixteen
A Very Splendor Christmas, Holiday Novella, Book
Seventeen
Paradise Point, Book Eighteen,
Silent Sunset, Book Nineteen
Rocky Basin, Book Twenty, Coming Next in the Series!

MacLarens of Fire Mountain

Tougher than the Rest, Book One
Faster than the Rest, Book Two
Harder than the Rest, Book Three
Stronger than the Rest, Book Four
Deadlier than the Rest, Book Five
Wilder than the Rest, Book Six

MacLarens of Boundary Mountain

Colin's Quest, Book One,
Brodie's Gamble, Book Two
Quinn's Honor, Book Three
Sam's Legacy, Book Four
Heather's Choice, Book Five
Nate's Destiny, Book Six
Blaine's Wager, Book Seven
Fletcher's Pride, Book Eight
Bay's Desire, Book Nine
Cam's Hope, Book Ten

Romantic Suspense

Eternal Brethren, Military Romantic Suspense

Steadfast, Book One
Shattered, Book Two
Haunted, Book Three
Untamed, Book Four
Devoted, Book Five
Faithful, Book Six
Exposed, Book Seven
Undaunted, Book Eight
Resolute, Book Nine
Unspoken, Book Ten
Defiant, Book Eleven, Coming Next in the Series!

Peregrine Bay, Romantic Suspense

Reclaiming Love, Book One
Our Kind of Love, Book Two
Edge of Love, Book Three, Coming Next in the Series!
Find all of my books at:
https://www.shirleendavies.com/books.html

About Shirleen

Shirleen Davies writes romance—historical, contemporary, and romantic suspense. She grew up in Southern California, attended Oregon State University, and has degrees from San Diego State University and the University of Maryland. Her passion is writing emotionally charged stories of flawed people who find redemption through love and acceptance. She now lives with her husband in a beautiful town in northern Arizona.

I love to hear from my readers!

Send me an email: shirleen@shirleendavies.com
Visit my Website: https://www.shirleendavies.com/
Sign up to be notified of New Releases:
https://www.shirleendavies.com/contact/
Follow me on Amazon:
http://www.amazon.com/author/shirleendavies
Follow me on BookBub:
https://www.bookbub.com/authors/shirleen-davies

Other ways to connect with me:

Facebook Author Page:
http://www.facebook.com/shirleendaviesauthor
Twitter: www.twitter.com/shirleendavies
Pinterest: http://pinterest.com/shirleendavies
Instagram:
https://www.instagram.com/shirleendavies_author/

Copyright © 2017 by Shirleen Davies

All rights reserved. No part of this publication may be reproduced, distributed, or transmitted in any form or by any electronic or mechanical means, including information storage and retrieval systems or transmitted in any form or by any means without the prior written permission of the publisher, except by a reviewer who may quote brief passages in a review. Thank you for respecting the hard work of this author.
For permission requests, contact the publisher.

Avalanche Ranch Press, LLC
PO Box 12618
Prescott, AZ 86304

Foolish Heart is a work of fiction. Names, characters, places, and incidents are either products of the author's imagination or used fictitiously. Any resemblance to actual events, locales, or persons, living or dead, is wholly coincidental.

www.ingramcontent.com/pod-product-compliance
Lightning Source LLC
Chambersburg PA
CBHW071744190726
48292CB00003B/864